Gem City

CONFIDENTIAL

J.P. Johnson

Lost Lake Folk Art

SHIPWRECKT BOOKS PUBLISHING COMPANY

Minnesota

IN®
DIE

For Erin, with much love.

Gem Gity

CONFIDENTIAL

Contents

Part I

1. Dead Girl

There was little comfort gained by repeating, "Her time was up." But the fatalists would say that. Parents told their kids the same thing at the supper table and teenagers whispered it to one another at school. Some others would say that she shouldn't have been out that late; carefully phrased so that it wouldn't sound like, if she hadn't been out late messing around, it wouldn't have happened.

As far as Barbara Benson knew, her time being up, was when she was finished working at the Qik Stop convenience store. At 10:30 p.m., she turned off some lights, cleared the cash register and placed the day's receipts and cash into a large envelope and slid them into the slot on top of the safe. Then, after one last glance, she locked the door.

Barbara was a senior at Gem City High School. After graduation, she hadn't decided what she would be doing, or whether or not she would be leaving Gem City. Someone else decided that at 12:20 a.m., Sunday, September 9th, 1966, she would be leaving Gem City.

The only one who decided that her time was up, was the person who offered to give her a ride home that night. She was mildly surprised that the one who picked her up, wasn't the person she'd expected, but it was all right, anyway. It was all right, just as long as it was someone familiar. Besides, she was only planning on going home.

The clearing in Penn's Woods was a well-known lovers' lane. For as long as anyone could remember—probably as long as high school boys asked to borrow their dads' cars—Penn's Woods was a popular make-out spot for local teens.

Located on the north end of town, Penn's Woods sprawled just across four lanes of asphalt known as the State Highway. Main Street, a wide two-laner, came up to the highway to form a T where a three-way semaphore allowed right or left turns. However, if you went straight across, the asphalt ended and twin dirt paths with a row of short grass in the middle would take you a couple hundred feet into pine tree and white birch seclusion.

On the way into the clearing and slightly off the path, barely space for one car, is were the lookout car parked. For about forty years, the last couple into the woods would back up into that space with the understanding that is the cops crossed the highway, the driver would honk the horn furiously. There was room in the clearing for three cars, if appropriately spaced, four, if not.

Every night, at about 11:30, the police would drive slowly into the clearing, turn the spotlight on and chase kids out, usually without a word being said. The next shift would come back, a little after the bars closed and chase the adults out.

On that clear, chill night, before he finished his shift, Sergeant Wickes drove his LTD cruiser around the clearing. No one was there, so he drove to the entrance, stopped and turned the headlights off. He smoked and waited till midnight and headed back to the station. His shift had been an unremarkable one, issuing only one parking ticket.

The shift change, at midnight, was basically a "hi, 'bye" affair between second and third shift cops. There was nothing much to report, so the third shift was handed the keys to the cruisers and that was it.

Officers, Dan Smith and Jeff Sikorski were on the midnight shift. Sikorski took the north end of town and Smith, the south end. An hour and a half into his shift, Sikorski entered Penn's Woods with his spotlight on. He began making a clockwise arc around the dusty clearing and stopped. He wasn't sure of what he saw at first, so he backed up a few feet, so that the spotlight and the headlights shone on the same object lying on the ground. He needed more light, grabbed a flashlight, and stepped out of the car.

As he slowly approached the object, he immediately recognized the lifeless form as the body of a young girl. She was lying face-down, wearing a heavy, red, wool sweater, black pants and a white shirt. Except for the sweater, it was the uniform everyone wore while clerking at the Qik Stop. "Aw shit, no," he whispered to himself. He felt a rush of adrenalin, blood pounded at his temples. His breathing became shallow and rapid. Sikorski sucked in the cool air deeply through his nostrils and exhaled in slow, measured bursts from his mouth. His breaths ended with almost a whistle and with the words, louder than before, "God—shit!"

Her arms were stretched out straight on either side of her blond head. Only her upper torso was in the clearing. Her legs, which lay in the thickening woods, were slightly apart. They looked as if they were dropped there.

Sikorski unsnapped his holster and with one hand on the stock of his .38, his finger sliding down alongside of the trigger, he scanned the clearing with his flashlight. He knelt on one knee close to the body. The right side of her face was visible between strands of her straight, blond hair. He shone his flashlight on her face and placed his left hand between her shoulder blades. With his right elbow on his right knee, he pointed his gun skyward.

No movement. It was then that he noticed her right eye was partially open. There were small flecks of dried blood around her nostril and her parted lips. *What the hell happened?* He looked at the dirt beyond her outstretched arms and noticed that of all the nearby tire tracks, only one set could've belonged to the vehicle that brought the victim to Penn's Woods.

He stood and waved the flashlight slowly up and down her body. He seemed almost amazed at the fact she was fully clothed, lying dead in Penn's Woods. *Wait a minute. Maybe an animal got a hold of her ... the two-legged kind. Oh, god!* He began to breathe deeply again and reaching for a cigarette, he saw that his hands were shaking.

Sikorski had seen much worse, like car accidents on the highway, but this was beginning to look like his first homicide and unlike a traffic accident, it called for a prescribed protocol. He radioed Smith and briefly explained the situation. The Chief, Bob Peterson, was to be called at home. He, in turn, would call the County Major Crimes Unit up in Saint Stephen. Lieutenant Dennis Hanson, of the Sheriff's Department and a couple of his deputies, would drive about thirty miles southeast to Gem City.

The other officer, "Smitty," picked up Peterson and drove to Penn's Woods with the "gumball machine" flashing red. When they joined Sikorski, the three of them smoked cigarettes and took turns cursing through their teeth and pacing. They shined flashlights on the body, but otherwise stood a few feet away. Finally, Chief Peterson asked Sikorski, "Well, who is, I mean, who was she? Did you check for ID? Homicide, huh?"

Before Sikorski could answer, a sheriff's car came barreling in on the dirt road. More red lights blazing. Lt. Hanson jumped out. Two other deputies strolled over to the Gem City cops. They all stood near the body, adjusting their gun belts. Hanson open the trunk, grabbed a spool of yellow crime scene tape and started wrapping it around a small bush.

Peterson shouted, "Christ, Hanson, don't you even say 'hi,' anymore?" Everybody but Hanson laughed. "You can wrap the other end of that tape around Smitty's schvantz," Peterson added. "There's a crime scene in itself!" The five cops howled while Hanson remained all business.

"Any ID on her?" Hanson asked, trying to restore some decorum. "Why don't you guys start looking for a purse or something, huh?"

"When's Shep coming?" Sikorski mumbled. Shep was Doctor Shephard, the County Coroner, or Medical Examiner, as he preferred to be called. Sikorski may as well have been talking to himself because nobody answered.

"Hey," one of the deputies called, as he lifted a pine branch with his arm, his flashlight pointed at the ground, "I've got something here!"

Hanson trotted over, "What you got?" The deputy pointed at a small, black shoulder bag. Hanson stuck out his hand and hissed, "Let's see it."

"Nothing like making it easy for ya, eh Hanson?" chided Peterson. He liked getting under Hanson's skin at every opportunity. But Hanson ignored Peterson's comments, as usual.

Hanson had a couple of years of college and made rank right away, while Peterson came up the ranks slowly. Besides, Hanson was a much younger man, about twenty-seven and solidly in the Sheriff's Department. Peterson, on the other hand, had to curry favor with whoever was the current Mayor of Gem City, whom he hoped would keep getting re-elected so that he could renew his contract as Gem City Chief-of-Police.

"Hang on now! Don't use your bare hand to pick up that purse," Hanson admonished the deputy. "Use your flashlight." Hanson put on a pair of thin, cotton gloves and cautiously opened the small purse as the others drew closer. "Empty. Goddamnit." He waved the purse around. "Okay, it's a long shot, but I'll have the lab look for prints … especially on the clasp."

"And you thought this was gonna be your lucky day," chortled Peterson. Hanson slipped the purse into a plastic bag without responding to Peterson's taunt.

Peterson tried a more serious tone. "No sense looking for tire tracks. Could be hundreds in here, including our own. I think she was being dragged into the woods and her killer, you know, meant to drag her farther into the woods but he was interrupted." Peterson's eyes darted around the scene. "Yeah, dragged her by the legs. Easier that way. Whoever killed her emptied the purse and gave it a fling."

Sikorski spoke up. "Okay, that's settled. When's Shep gonna get here?" he asked, as if Shep's arrival was the next logical point to bring up. Then he added another logical non sequitur. "Wish we had some coffee as long's we're waiting." The rest of them nodded in silent agreement.

"Smitty," Peterson motioned toward town. "Why don't you run down to the station and bring back six cups of coffee. Hell, just bring the whole damn pot and six cups."

"I'll take mine with cream and sugar," blurted Hanson, "I can't drink that thick muck the way you guys like it."

"You'll drink it black, like everybody else," Peterson mumbled.

Smitty turned to leave, then asked, "What about Shephard? He might want some coffee, too."

"Screw Shephard," snapped Peterson. "Let him bring his own coffee."

Hanson and Peterson walked alone to the back of Hanson's car.

Hanson: "Who was here before Sikorski?"

Peterson: "Wickes, Jerry Wickes. Why?"

Hanson: "Well, he might've seen something."

Peterson: "If he'd seen something, he would've said so. Sergeant Wickes has been here almost as long as I have. So if you're insinuating anything …"

Hanson: "What? Peterson, your cops keep such a tight schedule. I mean, Jesus, twice a night, you can set your watch. 11:30 and 1:30. C'mon. Whoever killed this kid was watching and waiting for Wickes to leave."

Peterson: "And she didn't know what they were waiting for?"

Hanson: "She didn't know the guy was gonna kill her, of course. What she and apparently everybody else knew, was once Wickes, or whoever, left this area at midnight, that another cop wouldn't be around till 1:30."

Peterson: "So, they had an hour and a half … "

Hanson: "To do whatever he wanted to her. Yeah."

2: Doctor Shephard

Peterson looked up from the ground, "I hear a car coming."

"It's Shephard

... finally," Hanson sighed. The medical examiner's car wheeled in, a thin cloud of dust rising through the headlights on a road so well-traveled there was hardly any dust to raise.

The car's silhouette, illuminated by a first quarter moon, looked like an ordinary, black Chevy station wagon, only the back roof was a bit taller than regular wagons. Shephard stopped a few feet into the clearing.

Shephard's assistant, a tall, thin young man with a grown-out flattened crewcut, climbed out first, reached back into the car and grabbed a large flash camera. Dr. Shephard made a grand entrance, as he always did, walking purposefully toward the crime scene without looking at anyone.

Hanson met him halfway. "Where've you been, Doc?" he asked breathlessly. "I mean, we got the call at the same time."

"She's not gonna be any more dead or alive on my account, is she?" replied Dr. Shephard. In his mid-fifties, Shephard was slightly, but only slightly, younger than Chief Peterson. "And don't call me Doc. It makes me sound old and senile. Don't call me Shep, either."

"Sorry, Dr. Shephard." Hanson pointed the way to the corpse, adding, "Looks like we've got a teen homicide."

Shephard gave Hanson a withering stare of condescension. "It's a homicide only if I say it's a homicide." Shephard adroitly ducked under the crime scene tape and motioned to his assistant. "There should be yellow tape at the entrance, too."

Chief Peterson swaggered over to Shephard. "How ya doin', Shep?"

"Just fine, Bob. Nice night."

Hanson's jaw dropped, Shephard's admonishment still fresh in his memory.

"What we have here, gentlemen," Shephard intoned, "is the start of a formal inquest into the murder of this poor girl. We'll be calling her Jane Doe, for now. What've we got for evidence, so far?"

"An empty purse." The laughter his comment elicited embarrassed Hanson.

"I want two shots of all four angles," Shephard told his assistant.

The white flash of camera blubs momentarily spotlighted everyone and everything in ghastly detail. Shephard squatted on his haunches.

"Stan, can you help me turn her over? She's in rigor and I want to see the other side of her face." Stan didn't look at the dead girl's face as he helped the Coroner. "Definite signs of trauma," Shephard said. "I can see three small wounds in her neck. Stan, come dawn, maybe Officers Smith and Sikorski can search the area for the murder weapon. If her purse was found, then the weapon might be around here someplace as well." The coroner continued in flat, slow tones. "She hasn't been lying here very long. No dew collected on her sweater, no fallen leaves on her. Which one of you … who was first on the scene? What time?"

Sikorski, certain of himself, replied, "I called Smitty at about 1:30. Right Smitty?"

Smitty nodded, "Sounds about right. Sure."

Shephard stood up, thinking aloud, "Let's see, it's now 3 a.m. I'd say she died approximately one hour before you found her, Sikorski." Still looking at the girl's body and without turning around, Shephard gestured with his thumb toward the black car. "Stan, do you wanna get the gurney and the bag?" The doctor's assistant left his camera next to the corpse … there'd be a few more pictures to take.

Shephard made a rolling motion with his arms. "Lay out the bag next to her and we'll roll her into it. Scratches and dirt on the left side of the face, consistent with being dragged a few feet. There's a bump on her forehead, probably post-mortem, also from being dragged. There's a little blood in the mouth, also in both nostrils. Curious, just plain curious." His voice trailed off, then came back stronger. "It looks like she's wearing a uniform or something. Here's a nametag—Barb B—Barb … B… Barbie." The wandering image of the teenage fashion doll startled Shephard. He blinked the thought away. "Barb … B." Shephard repeated slowly, putting more than enough space between the syllables.

"Urine stains at the crotch and inner thighs—still wet—bladder release before, or at the moment of death. Take some more pictures, Stan, before we zip her up. We'll need one of you deputies to help us lift her onto the gurney."

Shephard stopped to light a cigarette, flicked the match away and gazed at all the cops. "This is not to be leaked to anyone until the investigation is complete, understood?"

Smitty raised his hand. "How about if we leak that we found her alive, and with her last breath, she named the killer, you know, just to make the perp really nervous?"

They all started laughing, except Shephard, who gave Hanson a stern look.

Hanson shouted at Smitty, "All right, all right—listen, Dick Tracy, shut up until Shep, I mean Dr. Shephard, is done, okay?"

"I'll be giving her a complete autopsy as soon as I get some ID," Shephard said casually. "Until then, I'll just do a cursory exam. Goodnight gentlemen. Get some rest."

With Barb B.'s body loaded into the station wagon; Stan turned around and drove back to St. Stephen. The cops watched the taillights vanish into the night.

"What'll we do, now?" Peterson asked Hanson.

"Well, Shep is right about putting up a barricade and some more yellow tape at the entrance. Smitty and Sikorski can keep an eye on the area and search for that goddamn weapon that we'll never find. Let's go, you guys."

Hanson motioned to his deputies. "Peterson, I suppose when we finally ID her, you'll notify her parents?"

"I hope I can get some sleep before I have to do that," Peterson sighed. "G'night, Lieutenant, see ya around. Smitty, drive me home. Sikorski, plan on hanging around here for a while."

OOO

Stan and Dr. Shephard pulled into the lower-level parking lot outside one of the courthouse basement doors. The County Courthouse basement consisted of the morgue and the jail—in cozy proximity. The Sheriff's first floor office sat directly above both. The rest of the three-story courthouse was filled with courtrooms and county services offices. The Selective Service Office, home to the draft board, was safely ensconced in windowless offices on the top floor.

At the outside door of the lower level, the dead girl, zipped inside a canvas body bag strapped-down tight to the gurney, jiggled when the Coroner pushed her across the metal threshold.

"I suppose this could wait till tomorrow, but might as well get it over with," Shephard said. He and Stan laid out the body on a cold, stainless-steel exam table. Stan sat down with a clipboard to take notes.

The morgue was lighted in bright gray, fluorescent tones, making the scene seem surreal, grotesque, where even the living have a death-pallor. As if that wasn't enough, there was the nauseating mixture of Lysol, Pine Sol, bleach and ammonia, hanging over everything in the large room. Shephard donned thick rubber gloves and tied on a black rubber apron. He put on magnifying glasses, which looked like regular glasses except they made him look like the villain in some sci-fi yarn at a drive-in movie. Shephard lowered the clear Plexiglass eye shield.

He slipped the pair of white tennis shoes and white socks off her feet. Then took a shears and slit up one leg of the black, cotton pants, then the other. There was no belt, just an elastic waistband. White cotton panties came off with the pants. The shirt and sweater were similarly cut away, the cotton-polyester bra was sheared in the middle and the straps were cut, as well.

Shephard faced Stan and stated flatly, "We know the cause of death, but we know neither the motive, nor the instrument of death."

Stan's eyes widened. "'We know the cause …'" He wrote down each word as though it was the most profound word ever recorded.

Shephard wheeled a tray over to the table. On it were small, plastic envelopes and a jar of long cotton swabs, plus a few other items he was going to use.

"Except for a few incidental cuts and bruises, the body is in fairly pristine condition. With the exception of some dirt in her hair from being dragged across the ground, the hair appears to be recently washed … so does the rest of the body."

Stan was now taking notes furiously, keeping a tight grip on the side of the clipboard, while his mentor went on with his relentless monologue. "'… rest of the body,'" he whispered.

"I'll take a hair sample, the dirt from the scrapes on her face, blood sample ..." Shephard leaned in closer to examine the the small, wounds on the left side of the neck. "This is curious. They look like puncture wounds ... a narrow blade of some kind ... about nine-sixteenths-of-an inch-wide."

"A dagger or a knife?" Stan asked.

"I don't think so. The blade is too narrow, besides the edges are beveled on only one side."

"Could it be a letter opener?"

"This is too puzzling! It could be. On the other hand, one edge is flat! I can't figure out what it could be. All I know is that the wounds seem to have sealed when the blade was withdrawn. They look they were made in an upward angle and judging by the grouping, the wounds were made in quick succession.

"I want to see how deep the blade went."

Dr. Shephard took a long swab from a tray. "This wound here looks like it hit the hyoid bone and this one, the posterior digastric muscle. Ah, here's it is. This one destroyed her trachea. I'm able to go in about four-inches."

Both men came to the conclusion that she aspirated blood into her lungs when she gasped for air and therefore, suffocated, but not dying immediately, as they first thought.

He carefully scraped under the fingernails of both hands and placed the material in an envelope. Her fingerprints were also taken.

"Stan, you get to choose, Gigli Saw or the shears."

Stan chose the shears to make the pericardial cut.

3. Identification Confirmed

The phone rang, echoing loudly around the tiled walls. Shephard jumped back, startled. Stan's clipboard clattered to the floor. Stan leapt to his feet and loped toward the yellow wall phone.

"County Morgue. Yes, Chief, he's right here. It's Chief Peterson, sounds urgent."

Shephard took off his gloves and walked to the phone. "Yeah, Bob."

"I got a call, a few minutes ago, from someone whose daughter didn't come home last night. Their names are Ed and Stella Benson. I asked them to describe her and the description matched the girl we found."

"How can you be sure? She looks like a lot of girls."

"Because she was the only girl in town reported missing; that girl is lying in your morgue, right now. Her name is Barbara Benson. Didn't come home after work at the Qik Stop. I'm going over in a little while. Bringing Smitty."

"Have you told them anything yet?"

"No, not yet. That's why I'm gonna talk to them in person. God, maybe I can get some sleep tomorrow."

Peterson was good at delivering bad news, partly because he'd done it many times before and was therefore emotionally immune. Plus, he had eloquence and style, when he had to. He would stand on someone's front steps, his hat in his hands ... literally. He would briefly rehearse his part in the bathroom mirror before sunrise. When the Bensons' front light came on, it was showtime.

Shephard went back to his examination. He swabbed urine samples from the victim's thighs.

"Now, I'm going to swab the inside of her vagina ... looking for traces of semen, perhaps. Hmm, some fecal material, here. A little bowel release."

He spread her vagina and inserted a speculum. "Guess what, Stan? She's not a virgin. I don't think anybody is, anymore," he stated, looking over the top of his magnifying glasses.

Stan averted eye contact and stared at the clipboard. Shephard drew a vial of blood from the brachial artery located in the crook of her elbow.

"Well, we're done, for now. Let's get her into the cooler. By the way, Stan, did you ever hear of a so-called, scientific theory, that if you closely examined a victim's retinas you can see an image of the murderer? Like a photograph. That theory was actually put into practice in the late 1800's. I believe they tried it in the Jack the Ripper case, in England."

Stan nodded, pretending to be interested. The phone rang again. Shephard answered. It was Peterson again. "Shep, I just spoke to the Bensons. They took the news pretty hard. She was their only child. They both started sobbing. Stella went completely nuts. She was screaming and sobbing at the same time and collapsed in Ed's arms. Ed walked her to a chair and pushed her into it. I asked Ed to come by and ID the body, alone if possible, but they both insisted they'd do it together. As soon as they calm down, I'll bring them to the morgue. Be a couple of hours, at least. Have you heard from Hanson?"

"No."

"Well, I'll talk to him tomorrow, then. 'Bye, Shep. See ya later."

The Bensons arrived at 7:30 a.m. and confirmed their daughter's identity. Shep took some information from them, for the Death Certificate, and talked to them for a while. Chief Peterson overheard Shep tell them that the approximate time of death was midnight. Peterson has already told the Bensons there were no suspects yet, and that the police would begin looking first thing Monday morning. Ed Benson said that Lange and Whitehill's mortuary would come for his daughter's body.

OOO

Hanson drove down the next morning and met Peterson at the high school. He informed the Chief that the only prints on the purse were Barbara's. Peterson handled the introductions with teachers and staff. They commandeered the principal's office and began interviewing some of Barb Benson's teachers, friends and acquaintances. Barb evidently was not part of the in-crowd. A couple of the girls said that she was kind of a loner who didn't date much or attend school dances. She was an average student. The investigation bogged down from the very start. No suspects. No leads.

On the way out to their cars, Hanson asked Peterson, "Does that convenience store have any surveillance cameras?"

"They don't make enough money to have those things."

"Well, that's just great." Hanson sighed with resignation.

There would be a lot of sighing in the days to follow.

The Qik Stop stayed closed for an entire week. On Monday, Hanson examined the cash register receipts going back to Saturday night.

On Tuesday, Peterson's phone rang. It was Shephard. He sounded excited. "The lab results came in and guess what? She was pregnant. Not very far along, perhaps only about three weeks, or less. I just told Hanson and I thought he was gonna piss his pants."

"Pregnant? This may well be a motive. The father, if we can identify him, becomes our prime suspect. Call Hanson back and tell him to zip it."

"Will do. Hanson's got to keep quiet about this."

They might've gone to Penn's Woods to talk about the pregnancy, Peterson mused to himself. One thing led to another. She said the wrong thing and bingo. The murderer was someone she knew very well. Peterson personally hoped the father was someone outside Gem City. The more Peterson thought about this case, the more he thought about the news, how word of the grizzly murder was not going to stay within the city limits, not the county limits either; the more he thought about retiring.

Chief Peterson, Dr. Shephard and Sheriff's lieutenant Hanson all agreed that for the foreseeable future, the fact that Barb Benson was pregnant would be kept secret, even from her parents.

4: Bob, Dennis, Ed and Stella

Peterson came to Gem City after World War Two, to answer a help wanted ad in the Minneapolis *Journal*. Apparently, whoever wrote the ad made Gem City sound quite appealing. Peterson took the job, first as a patrolman, then sergeant, and five years as Chief. He and his wife raised a son and a daughter in a story-and-a-half home in Gem City purchased with a G.I. Bill zero-down mortgage in 1947.

Even before the Benson case, he had occasionally thought about retiring, but the Benson case was likely going to be the last straw. The Chief really wanted to move back to Minneapolis—maybe get an office job for some, big security guard firm.

The kids were both away at the University of Minnesota. His wife, Ruthie, didn't even wake up anymore when the phone rang in the middle of the night for some police emergency. There was always an emergency, it seemed, in the middle of the night.

Working all-hours as Chief-of-Police was taking more of a toll on Peterson than on Ruthie. She was happy that he became Chief. The money was good, and he had other people on the Force to pick up body parts after accidents on the state highway. That hadn't always been the case.

When he first started his job, he had to arrest Margaret Schneider for murder. Margaret's husband, Carl, who worked second shift at the foundry, was a roaring, physically abusive drunk. Carl worked till midnight, and by the time he came home, usually around three a.m., he'd tear into Margaret—beat the shit out of her—threaten to kill her. He was a mean drunk.

One morning, after the kids went to school, she decided that she'd had enough. At about nine a.m., she went down to the basement and pretended to have a good time by singing. Carl didn't like Margaret having a good time, especially when it didn't involve him and, more often than not, it didn't. He also didn't like to be awakened before noon. So that morning, he jumped out of bed, mad as hell, and ran down the basement steps determined to give Margaret the beating of her life. Margaret greeted Carl at the bottom of the basement stairs with Carl's 12-gauge shotgun. The barrel couldn't have been more than a foot away from his face when she squeezed the trigger. Peterson remembered going over there and picking up pieces of Carl's skull, some, no bigger than a nickel. scattered about, on the stairway. It was a direct hit, leaving only his lower jaw intact. The overpowering wet stink of excrement, urine and blood rose out of his corpse.

Patrolman Bob Peterson carefully took the shotgun from Margaret, leaned it against the wall and applied handcuffs. She tried to say something, but nothing came out. He had nothing to say either. She had a vacant, haunted look in her eyes, exactly the kind of look he'd seen while fighting in the Pacific during the war. They called it, "the thousand-yard stare."

Margaret was prosecuted in Saint Stephen District Court by a County Attorney. Neighbors were called as witnesses to Carl's behavior. Gem City police chief at the time, Elmer Baaken, testified that Carl had been jailed many times for spousal abuse. Baaken said, as others did, that Margaret had simply had enough, and that Carl got what he deserved. Margaret's attorney tried to enter an insanity plea. Times being what they were, she was convicted of First-Degree Murder, which was reduced to Second-Degree on appeal. The last Bob Peterson heard, Margaret had served some time at the women's prison in Shakopee, then disappeared.

Bob Peterson was tired. The fact that he was happy to have Dennis Hanson from the Sheriff's Office working on the Benson murder was a sure sign of fatigue. If the case wasn't solved soon, he resolved to announce his retirement. Then he wondered to himself, *What would happen to Smitty? What if the new chief let Smitty go for being occasionally dense, or for being a dipshit most of the time? If that's what's going to happen, I'll just have to recommend Smitty to become Chief-of-Police then.*

OOO

Barbara's funeral would be held on Saturday morning at Saint Stephen Lutheran Church, a week after her murder, so that relatives from out of town could arrive. She would be buried at Gethsemane Cemetery, Gem City's only active cemetery—non-denominational, of course.

One of the strangest things about the cemetery was that though the city owned it, Lange and Whitehill Funeral Home leased the

18

graveyard, and they, in turn, sold burial plots to the families of decedents. The undertaker's partnership with the city ensured that money would seldom be circulated outside of Gem City.

Lange and Whitehill opened the largest room in their chapel for reviewal Barbara on Friday night.

Irish Catholics held wakes. Scandinavian Lutherans were more stoic and reserved. They had reviewals—they reviewed the body. If everything looked okay, they would go ahead and bury it. The good Christian people of Gem City believed cremation, on the other hand, to be a Communist plot to keep Americans from getting into heaven.

On Friday night, cops in plain clothes descended on the funeral home. Lt. Hanson, three deputies, Chief Peterson and four patrolmen, all of them watched steely-eyed as people arrived at the reviewal. It's a well-worn theory that homicidal maniacs often attend the funerals of their victims.

Old couples, middle-aged couples, teenaged couples and singles, poured into the funeral home, which was a hideous hodgepodge of Greek, Roman and Southern antebellum architecture. A continually buzzing pink neon sign, in script lettering reading, "Lange and Whitehill Funeral Home," greeted people as they filed into the main entrance. No one knew and no one asked why Lange's name appeared in smaller letters, but at least he got top billing.

The reviewal was an informal gathering of friends and relatives of the deceased. They sat and talked and stood around and talked. The cops circulated among the mourners. Barbara Benson, or rather her body, was dressed in a black skirt and a high-necked white blouse. Around her neck, she wore a small, gold cross on a delicate gold chain.

The next morning, Barbara Benson moved closer to eternity. High school kids crammed the balcony of the church. There was room on the main floor, but they wanted to sit together and away from their parents and teachers. For someone for whom it was said, "she didn't have any friends," Barbara drew a sizeable crowd. Perhaps a lot of them were only curious.

The cops eyeballing the attendees also eyeballed cars outside in the parking lot. They nervously smoked cigarettes. Maybe the murder took place inside one of those cars. Maybe the asshole was inside the church.

The hearse, a black Cadillac, stood alone close to the front doors of the church.

The church organ, with pipes imported from Switzerland, belted out an ancient dirge. A pimply-faced girl sang in a high, thin, wispy voice backed by a male friend on acoustic guitar— some pop song doubling as a funeral hymn. After that, the organist pounded out the more traditional, *Rock of Ages*, which could be heard for blocks beyond the huge parking lot.

Exactly an hour after it started, the funeral was over. Barbara Benson's white casket with pink trim was carefully pushed into the hearse as the mourners followed Barbara's parents out.

Odd that Stella Benson, Barb's mother, walked right past the hearse without looking or pausing—she just kept walking. Most of the crowd gathered around the hearse, some patting Ed Benson on his back and shoulders. Ed noticed Stella walking toward their car. They were supposed to drive it in the funeral procession, behind the hearse. Ed didn't understand why Stella was in such a rush to get going. He excused himself and walked briskly to catch up to her. Ed was about eight feet behind Stella when she wheeled around with a .22 revolver clasped in a two-handed shoulder point position.

"You!" she screamed and started firing. The first two shots went wild and ripped into the side of the stucco church, scattering the horrified crowd.

Cops were yelling, "Get back inside!"

A couple of officers followed Chief Peterson to positions behind the hearse. The third shot passed through Ed's trachea and out the back of his neck. The fourth and fifth shots were much more lethal. One bullet pierced his stomach, doubled him over and spun him around in a macabre pirouette. When he turned, she shot him in the lower back. He fell to his knees, then onto his side, still doubled up, lying there on the asphalt, gasping—the only sound he made.

Every time she fired, she took a couple of paces backward, legs apart, focused. She didn't notice the stunned deputies crouching, their .38s drawn. A couple of them had .357s. When Lt. Hanson opened up, three more guns started firing at Mrs. Benson. She spasmed violently. They kept firing until her knees buckled. She crumpled and fell heavily, lifeless, flat on her back. She lay there,

eyes wide open, legs and arms twisted in horrible positions—
blood everywhere, people screaming—cops running toward the
carnage.

Dr. Shephard later determined that Stella Benson had been shot
a total of twenty times in the upper torso, including a few shots to
the head, neck and face. She died at the scene. Ed was still
breathing when Chief Peterson reached him and called for an
ambulance.

It was a bad day all around for the Bensons, as well as for the
Sixth Commandment. Fifteen minutes after Stella fired the first
shot, a Gem City ambulance delivered Ed to Gem City's small
hospital a few blocks south.

OOO

Lt. Hanson and a couple of his men sat on metal folding chairs
in a sky-blue waiting room drinking black coffee and smoking
cigarettes until a sullen-faced doctor came in and told Hanson that
he could ask Ed a few questions. "Only a few questions."

Hanson and his deputies marched down the hall to Ed's room.
Hanson was mildly surprised when he discovered, at least in that
moment, he actually had a fairly decent bedside manner.

"Ed, you don't have to answer any questions if you don't want
to, but I want you to know that things don't look very good for
you. We've got two crimes to work on now."

Ed's eyes were open. He squinted at the ceiling. There was a
trach-tube in his neck, an oxygen cannula under his nose and a
bottle of fluid dripping through an IV into his arm.

"His larynx was shattered," said the doctor in a flat monotone.
He gestured toward Ed, "I'm afraid Mr. Benson's will not able to
talk."

Hanson repeated the word *larynx* to himself before posing his
first question. "Ed, what can you tell us? What was going on
between you and your wife? Why the hell did she try to kill you? I
should tell you, your daughter was pregnant, Ed."

Ed looked right and left at the walls, then lay there blinking at
the ceiling again. Finally, he peered at Hanson.

"Do you know who killed Barb?"

Ed nodded affirmatively and made a hissing sound through clenched teeth.

"Nurse." Hanson interrupted the young RN who happened to be checking the IV bottle. "Can you crank up his bed a little?" Hanson moved closer to Ed's pallid face.

"Here's a pad and pen. Can you write the name of the person you think did it?"

Hanson steadied the small notebook as Ed feebly tried to write. He started making a large letter. His hand shook. The letter he drew arched then curved downward before disappearing off the page. Ed dropped his hand, still clutching the pen. Hanson quickly took the notebook away and stared at the mark Ed drew.

The nurse quickly checked for Ed's pulse. "I think he's dead, Doctor."

The doctor nodded and sternly glared at Hanson. "I guess you boys can leave now," he said sardonically.

"Okay, and I guess he can keep the pen," Hanson replied, his temporary bedside manner gone.

Hanson walked out with the two deputies and started down the white hallway when he suddenly stopped and asked both men, "What do you make of this?" He slapped the notebook with the back of his hand. "What's it supposed to be? An S? A snake? A backwards question mark?"

5. Dennis Hanson, Gem City and the War

The weather abruptly turned cold. TV and radio weathermen said the cold snap was unseasonable and unforeseen, but everyone knew better. The only thing certain was death and taxes—not Minnesota weather, especially in the Fall.

Toward late September, when it wasn't raining, the dark sky threatened rain. Then it would rain some more. By late October, the rain turned to sleet. The sleet eventually became snow. It usually happened that way, so it really wasn't unpredictable. Gem City measured snow not in inches but in feet. When Gem City got dumped on, the town would be inevitably paralyzed for half a day, sometimes longer.

Bob Peterson retired on January 2nd, 1967, after twenty-one years as a Gem City cop. He and Ruthie moved to South Minneapolis. Bob got a desk job with Pinkerton's and they bought a four-bedroom house. The kids moved into the house but weren't thrilled about leaving their dorm rooms. It was for the best—tuition costs were rising.

About a year later, Lt. Hanson marked the Barbara Benson case "CLOSED". It ended as cold as it began—no suspects, no leads. A family dead. Hanson felt the tragic case might never be solved, but there was nothing more he could do.

Promotion to Captain 9 months after the Benson murder meant Hanson could settle into more of an administrator role at the Sheriff's Department, which meant he wouldn't have to leave his office every time a major crime was committed. One day in 1968, there was a bank robbery at one of Gem City's two banks. Other banks in nearby towns were also hit within a day or two. Captain Hanson suspected serial robberies, so he personally drove into Gem City. FBI jurisdiction in the bank robberies meant that Hanson was more or less a bystander until one of the agents asked the Sheriff's Captain to stay and help out. Hanson took the request as an insult but stayed long enough to discuss the evidence. He felt confident that the FBI, not the Sheriff's Department, would quickly solve the string of bank hold-ups.

Dennis Hanson eventually married. Divorce followed a couple of years later. Since it wasn't officially called "divorce" in Minnesota, the marriage was officially dissolved. "Means the same damn thing!" Hanson complained to his divorce attorney. He ran for County Sheriff twice and lost twice, but he kept his job as Captain and stayed with the Major Crimes Unit.

Not long after the Benson case turned cold, Dr. Shephard and his assistant Stan were transporting a corpse to the morgue when a car-full of college students from St. Cloud broadsided them on a city street in St. Stephen. There were no survivors.

It turned out that there were no survivors in the Gem City Police Department after Chief Peterson retired. The following January, Gem City Council decided that maintaining a police force of any size would no longer be economically feasible because of a steady decrease in population. Instead, Gem City contracted with the county to provide police services.

Gem City kept the volunteer Fire Department, whose members doubled as police reservists when the situation warranted. But other city services had to be scaled back to keep the firefighters. The mayor and city councilmembers reasoned that cutbacks were necessary to ease the burden on taxpayers. In the election that followed, Gem City's elected officials were overwhelmingly re-elected.

OOO

All the while the Vietnam War raged on. When President Lyndon Baines Johnson came before the American people with a heavy heart, it meant that we—Americans—were getting our asses kicked over in Southeast Asia. Johnson was getting his ass kicked over here, too as the War gained in disfavor.

Eight recent graduates of Gem City High School were killed in Nam. The mothers of those eight young men agreed to send Johnson letters asking him why he killed their sons and how many more mothers' sons would have to die before he put an end to the War. The President popped a nitro tablet under his tongue and signed a response to the Gem City mothers' letter promising that the hostilities in Vietnam would soon end. Six men and one young woman, an Air Force nurse, came home to Gem City unscathed.

Some people would say that the War got much worse when

Johnson declined to run for a second term and Richard Milhouse Nixon was elected. When Nixon's secret plan to end the War didn't materialize, folks in Gem City started referring to him informally as "that fuckin' Nixon". Eventually, the War ended like preceding wars had. A few fighters came home to Gem City and a few did not.

Part II

6. In the Beginning

In the seventeenth century, French fur traders made use of the Mississippi River and its currents as a major trade route from what the Dakota tribes called Minnesota all the way down to Louisiana, named for a French King.

In April 1680, Father Louis Hennepin braved the Upper Mississippi River in flat-hulled boats with his entourage of monks and Voyageurs; from the late seventeenth century until the late nineteenth, Voyageurs transported furs to Montreal traders. Hennepin's mission was two-fold, to explore the region, and to convert heathen natives to Christianity.

The river made a gradual turn to the southeast where the city of St. Stephen would eventually be built. At the slight crook in the river, flowing southwest then back to the southeast, Gem City would one day be founded. It was there, at the bend, that Hennepin's party carefully maneuvered their boats close to the rocky shoreline. They dropped anchors and waded through knee-deep water in order to let the men stand or squat behind scrub pines to relieve themselves.

Father Hennepin tipped his head back so that the hood of his brown, wool cloak slid off and settled onto his shoulders. He stood with one foot on a rock and scanned what looked to him like an alien landscape. On the west side of the river stood a tall, sheer cliff layered in gray shale and limestone. Pines of various heights looked down at him from atop the ridge. The east side, where they moored their boats, appeared terraced as the land gradually left the riverbank and rolled upward at about a thirty-degree angle toward higher plains. Through the thin forest of pines, oaks and birch, Hennepin could see where the land flattened out, about a mile away.

After the men finished with their bodily functions, they looked at Hennepin for guidance. He shrugged in disgust and started to stumble back toward the boats, mumbling, *"Pas ici."* Not here. He repeated it louder and clearer, *"Pas ici!"* Hennepin's men began to scramble toward the boats. Then, inexplicably, he held up his hand

and stopped. Turning back to the east again, he commanded one of the monks to bring him his cross. The monk scurried to a boat and produced a gold cross, encrusted with *fleurs de lis* on each of its three points, a small reproduction of a huge cross Hennepin kept in a monastery in Quebec. The monk placed the cross in the good Father's hands. Hennepin raised the cross upward toward the plateau and intoned some Latin oath or another before handing the cross back to the monk and telling him to tell the others that they would continue onward down the river.

They had to be sharp and especially watchful of the changing currents, the colossal, smooth, gray and black boulders in the middle of the river, and the dead, sun-bleached tree limbs clinging to shores and sandbars. Some of them, with a little imagination, looked like the skeletal remains of pterodactyls.

Hennepin and his haggard crew steered cautiously down the river about a hundred miles. They slowed as they came to a great widening bend in the river. The group landed on the hospitable-looking south bank. Father Hennepin got out of his boat, knelt on the sandy shore and made the sign of the cross. His fellows did the same.

No sooner than that was accomplished, they were surrounded and outnumbered by Sioux Braves who stood motionless, their arrows pointed at the terrified Frenchmen. The Indians seized Hennepin's boats and started marching the confused men to their village, a short distance away near an area that would later be known as Fort Snelling.

To the foreigners, the Indians were pleasantly cordial, inviting the explorers to what turned into a summer-long hunting and feasting party. A couple of voyageurs went back to the supply boat and rolled barrels of red wine to the Sioux camp to enhance the festivities. So, the foreigners sunbathed, ate venison, and drank wine until they were lost in delirium.

Then, on one sunny morning, fellow explorer, Graysolon du Lhut, came paddling to shore. "Hennepin!" he shouted, "I am here to rescue you!"

"Rescue me from what?" was Hennepin's reply. Eventually, they packed up their boats, bid *adieu* to their Indian brethren and paddled farther down The Big Muddy.

Hennepin would later boast that he had discovered the mouth of the Mississippi, but the Sioux knew better and soon everyone else knew that Hennepin fabricated that story.

Surveyors and cartographers from New York, descended on the newly formed Minnesota Territory in 1849. They measured and mapped from trees to boulders, from rivers to lakes and from the lowlands to the highlands, utilizing what is termed, the metes-and-bounds survey method.

That same year, the new territory lost a few of its settlers to the lure of gold discovered in California. Others, from the eastern seaboard cities, rumbled by on horses, mules, oxen or, whatever carried them across the Great Plains. They neither cared nor noticed that Minnesota offered squatters' rights to new homesteaders.

Along the Mississippi River, about a hundred miles north of Saint Paul, Saint Stephen Township covered an area of thirty-six square-miles, a four square-mile portion of which was incorporated as the Village of St. Stephen, which later became known as the City of St. Stephen as well as the County Seat. No one was sure where they got the name, St. Stephen. Some said that it was named of an ancient Hungarian king.

In the southwest corner of the township, German, Slavic and Scandinavian settlers occupied two and one-half square-miles incorporated a second Village for St. Stephen. The territorial government intervened, and the smaller village reluctantly agreed to rename itself the Village of St. Stephen Point, which was later renamed Gem City to no objection.

The Sinclair family first settled in St. Stephen Township in 1880. They had a hundred-acre farm. In order to facilitate ingress and egress, the Sinclairs carved out a wagon trail about four-hundred feet from the front door of their white, two-story home.

As more families came and built farms not far from the Sinclairs, the trail was widened and lengthened. The farms raised cows, chickens, pigs and horses. Farmers grew wheat, potatoes, corn and all kinds of vegetables. The soil was very good for growing things because it had a thick, rich topsoil of the blackest dirt anyone had ever seen.

Geologists would later say that the black dirt was actually volcanic ash spread over the Midwest by a super volcano that had erupted eons ago somewhere in the Northwest Pacific Rim. They say the super volcano is what drove the dinosaurs to extinction. Other scientists called the theory nonsense, arguing that the black soil was created when mammoth forest fires swept across the North American plains. Still other scientists insisted that the soils were caused by a gigantic glacier, which plowed through the region and turned the soil over. The farmers, however, didn't care one way or another so long as seasonal crops filled their lofts, silos and root cellars.

A few Irish families followed the other immigrants to St. Stephen. Among them, the Murphys, who sharecropped on the Penn farm. The long trail now had a north end to it, angling slightly toward the farm owned by the Penns.

The Murphy family had emigrated from Ireland via Boston, consisting of Mr. Murphy, his wife, and their fourteen-year old son, Joel. The Penns had lumber leftover after building their barn, and they gave it to the Murphys to build their house. In the new Minnesota territory, ancient European animosities were put aside for later, perhaps forever.

In the late 1800s and early 1900s, immigrants started coming through the gates of Ellis Island in droves. After they were unceremoniously deloused, they met real estate entrepreneurs who were willing to sell them farmland in the North Central United States in general, Minnesota, in particular. The immigrants were assured that the climate was every bit as temperate as their former homelands, and they would be able to grow any crop they wanted. Many came and settled in St. Stephen. Thus, the long trail was again widened and lengthened and eventually dubbed, Main Street.

Norwegians settled in the smaller Village of St. Stephen Point, where they established the first church, St. Stephen Lutheran. This raised considerable concern and anguish among the predominately Catholic citizens of the village, who were planning to build a Catholic church and naming it Saint Stephen's Catholic. They argued that Saint Stephen was a Catholic and that Lutherans should not go around naming Protestant churches after Catholic saints. Further, the Catholics vehemently asserted that the Township was named for Hungarian King Stephen I, who spent most of his life battling pagan rebels. In the year 998, he and his army of reformers routed the pagans at Veszprem. Again in 1030, he defeated an invasion by Emperor Conrad. Stephen I was canonized in 1083.

The Lutherans conceded that perhaps the township was named after the Catholic Saint Stephen but remained smug in their assertion that the Lutheran church would remain St. Stephen after an early Christian convert and martyr. Their Saint Stephen was a Jew who professed that Moses, himself, had prophesized the coming of Jesus as the Messiah. Stephen was stoned to death for blasphemy. And so began the rivalry between the two churches.

The Lutheran church held services in the basement until the superstructure was completed in 1898, a year before the Catholics began construction on their church. The Lutherans felt they could claim the name, St. Stephen. The Catholics, maybe for spite, built their church right across the street and named it, Our Lady of the River.

The Baptists didn't build a church until 1926 and built it on the south end of Main Street. They called it Main Street Baptist. The Methodists started their church in 1940. After an argument with the Catholics, they named their church, St. Mark's.

Each church, except for St. Mark's, had a cemetery. The Lutherans dedicated a half-acre next-door to the church. The Catholics consecrated a full acre a few blocks to the east of their church on top of a hill. They surrounded the property with a high, wrought-iron fence. The Catholic cemetery looked odd because it sat vacant for nearly a decade. Due to their modest-sized congregation, the Baptists blessed an equally modest-sized cemetery adjacent to their humble church—about forty by one-hundred feet.

7. Joel Murphy Becomes a Penn

Rather than bother the Penns to use their well, Mr. Murphy sank his own well next to his house. Mr. and Mrs. Murphy contracted cholera and died in their beds. Their son, Joel, remained miraculously untouched by the disease. Joel was allowed to stay with the Penns.

A doctor came down from the county and declared the little house quarantined. Then, he and old-man-Penn burned the house to the ground, along with the bodies of the Murphys and all their clothes and possessions. All that remained, besides a pile of ashes, was the stone and mortar chimney, which was soon knocked down with sledgehammers. The priest and a few congregants from Our Lady of the River came to the smoldering heap to pray for the Murphys' souls. The ashes were covered over with black dirt and grass was planted. The Penns sprang for a granite marker with the names and vital statistics of the Murphys chiseled into it.

Joel Murphy, almost a grown man by then, was put to work as a hired hand for the Penns. It was anybody's guess how many acres the Penns owned, but it was the largest and most successful farm in the entire county. Some said it was well over a thousand acres. They had quite a few hired hands, but Joel was the Penn's favorite, so they made him foreman over all the others.

Old-man and old-lady-Penn were childless, and because they were getting up in years they decided, when they felt the time was right, to adopt Joel. Joel had his last name changed to Penn.

When old-man and old-lady-Penn people died a few years later, Joel inherited everything—the whole empire plus about a million in cash, which the deceased Penns had told Joel was hidden under the floor boards in the parlor of the house.

Joel Penn founded the first bank in St. Stephen Point. His bank did a brisk business and had depositors and borrowers from all over the county. He also became a real estate broker. Joel platted-out the Penn farm into one-hundred-foot frontage lots and had roads cut into the property. While still young, Joel made a fortune selling the lots for fifty dollars apiece to people who wanted to be gentlemen farmers, farmers without the work. He sold some of the lots to the men who used to be hired hands on the very same property. He saved a few acres, about ten, around his adopted parents' graves, then began selling burial plots to anyone who wanted a non-denominational, eternal resting place.

Joel was rich, and was just getting started. He went down to Minneapolis and begged the railroad to run their line over toward the river and alongside St. Stephen Point. The railroad obliged, by veering along the river and acquiring a half-square mile of the town's western border—right down to the river.

It turned out very well for the farmers who could ship their produce and livestock to the Twin Cities, and it was good for the merchants who could import dry goods. When the passenger line was added, the railroad built a handsome depot and called it Union Station.

With everything going so well, Penn decided to open a saloon on Main Street, a two-story, rectangular building with a huge apartment above, which he kept for himself but seldom occupied.

He made frequent trips to Minneapolis. While there, he asked local entertainers if they would consider performing at his saloon. Whenever they balked, he would simply offer them more money. There was one man he almost hired, thin and wiry, who sang and tap danced. It was a novelty act in that the man had a false leg sewn to the crotch of his pants. The false leg also had a tap shoe on the end of it. So, when he danced, the audience could hear three shoes tapping.

He passed on that act and hired instead an Italian tenor who played the accordion.

Joel became more interested in running the saloon than being a banker or a real estate mogul. He sold the bank to a man named Lewis and sold his real estate interests to Mr. Dunn.

Dunn re-platted the unsold property on the old Penn farm into forty-by-sixty-foot lots, and by the time Halley's Comet streaked by in 1910, St. Stephen Point's population had blossomed to seven-hundred—almost as large as the metropolis up river, the City of St. Stephen.

One morning, tragedy struck at the saloon. A railroad man got into an argument with a townie over who was buying the next round of hooch. The railroad man pulled a knife, so the townie pulled out a long-barreled revolver and started shooting. Bullets flew everywhere and the few customers in the saloon sought refuge by hitting the deck or crawling under the heavy, oak tables. The railroad man remained unscathed. A couple of bullets went through the front window and struck Jimmy Buttweiller, a fifteen-year old newsboy who was crossing Main Street; getting ready to hawk the *Bugle*, the local weekly newspaper. Jimmy took one bullet in the forehead and fell face-first into the dry, dusty, wheel-rutted street. The boy's name appeared in the *Bugle*, the following week.

Penn was upstairs in bed when he heard the commotion. It wasn't the sound of the gunfire that concerned him, it was the percussion of shots being fired inside his saloon. He grabbed a loaded shotgun, which he kept under his bed, and ran down the steps, still in his nightgown.

"What the hell's goin' on down here?" he yelled.

The smell of burnt gunpowder hung heavy in the air. The silent crowd all pointed fingers at the railroad man and the townie. Penn gestured toward the door with the shotgun barrel.

"All right, everybody out except you two birds. You men put your weapons on the floor and move back against the wall!"

"Kowalski," he shouted to his bartender, "run upstairs and use my telephone to call the sheriff. Tell him to bring the wagon. And then go over and get Sad Bill, the undertaker, to attend to young Buttweiler. Hurry up!"

Joel's again focused on the two men who stood there trembling. The railroad man was a huge, red-faced Irishman named Jake Riley. The townie was nearly a head shorter than Riley. His name was Earl Watson. Penn, his voice lower now, more in control, barked, "Godammit, you fellas! This is a quiet, peaceful town and this is a nice establishment. I spent a lot of money to make it that way and you two had to come along. I'm sick of you railroad bastards comin' in here and bustin' up the place. And you, Watson, you murdered that kid."

"I didn't mean to," Watson said.

Penn raised his shotgun, "Just shut the hell up, I didn't ask you to say anything. The sheriff should be here in about a couple of hours and anything you two have to say, you can say to him."

For weeks afterward, the increasing level of lawlessness in town disturbed Joel Penn. He was concerned about the impact the recent tragedy could have on his business. So, he approached the village council and stated that they ought to hire a police force. The council agreed and hired four hulking brutes, two Irish and two Poles, to keep the peace.

The officers took turns being Chief, which brought a slight increase in pay. Eventually, one of the men considered for the job of Chief turned out to be Jake Riley, the railroad man with the knife. Penn, the wealthiest man in town, strenuously objected and threatened to close the saloon if the Irishman was named Chief. Joel addressed the village council in an effort to make the council see things his way.

"Gentlemen, I don't know why you like this Jake Riley so much. Maybe it's because he was fired from the railroad and you feel sorry for him. That's no excuse to hire him as a policeman and name him Chief. After all, he was the one who started the fight that got Jimmy Buttweiler killed. Why, Jimmy might've been elected President of these United States one day."

"Mr. Penn, sir, you know as well as the rest of us that the Buttweiler boy wasn't right in the head."

"Well, then," Penn replied, "he would've made as fine a President as we have ever elected." When muted laughter and snickers subsided, Joep Penn continued. "I'm here to recommend Jimmy's father, Ernest Buttweiler. Ernest'll make sure that Riley and people like him stay out of my bar and out of this town."

"But, Mr. Penn, Ernest Buttweiler is nothing but a drunken, thieving hooligan. Been that way since his wife ran off with a horse collar salesman."

"That's exactly why you're gonna hire him. It's better to have him with us than against us."

The village council voted unanimously to hire Ernest Buttweiler as its newest police officer.

8. Gem City, Joel Penn and Ada Nesterud

T he population having doubled in 1916, the village council voluntarily disbanded in favor of St. Stephen Point becoming an incorporated city. The election of mayor and four city councilmembers was tabled until a new name for the city could be chosen. The name of St. Stephen Point had become tiresome, and anyway, it reminded people too much of the St. Stephen upriver. It also reminded them of the time that St. Stephen had stolen the name out from under them in the first place. So, they had a naming contest, the winner of which would receive a twenty-dollar gold piece and their name in the *Bugle*. There would be no second or third place—only first place.

Entries came in by the hundreds. Names such as, Columbia, Mississippi City, Lincolnville, Lewistown (probably submitted by the Lewis') and, preposterously, Pennsylvania. Joel Penn always denied entering the contest.

Unexpectedly, the winning entry came from nine-year-old Jeanne Halvorson, who submitted the name, Gem City. The reason, she explained, was that once, while she was playing in her front yard, "I saw some green pieces of glass from a broken wine bottle and thought they were emeralds. And at night, I look at the sky and the stars are like diamonds, and the sunset sometimes looks like a big, red ruby being swallowed by the cliff on the other side of the river, and the sky before sunrise looks like … "

"Here," interrupted a member of the contest committee, "take the twenty-dollars with our appreciation and go home." Jeanne hadn't even gotten to her sapphires and topazes analogy; her parents already had the money spent on a new barn.

Joel Penn was asked to run for mayor in the city's first election, but as expected he declined. One of the hulking Irish brutes, Samuel McConnell, formerly employed as a policeman, ran unopposed and was elected to a two-year term. Herb Sinclair, Alf Erickson, George Riley and Elmer Anderson were elected to four-year council terms.

Around this time, automobiles were becoming more prevalent, so Herb Sinclair bought a choice piece of land on the south end of Main Street and built a filling station. He called it "Sinclair's Standard Oil".

In writing the city charter, the newly elected authors decided to include a recall provision. In Gem City's first ever recall, Sinclair was removed from office under the charges of influence peddling and conflicts of interest. An additional but unrelated charge of contributing to the delinquency of a minor, was included.

Eight candidates filed for Gem City's first ever special election. A nineteen-year old man named Augie Schmidt was elected.

According to the charter, councilmembers were elected in staggered terms, which, ironically, meant that Joel Penn's saloon would be closed every time there was an election. Penn estimated that he would lose nearly a thousand dollars every election.

Things were beginning to look darker for Mr. Penn. Then, in the 1920 council election, suffragette, Mrs. Ada Nesterud was elected in a landslide. Mrs. Nesterud lost her husband in France during World War One. He wasn't killed, he just never returned to the United States.

Ada Nesterud never suffered fools gladly. She threatened to shut down Penn's saloon along with the bawdy entertainment he provided. Perhaps Ada was the way she was because rumor had it that Erroll Nesterud, her missing husband, got himself hooked-up with a Parisian entertainer. In any event, Ada believed that liquor and entertainment were not a good mix for married men.

Mrs. Nesterud's stout and matronly stature, as well as her cherubic face and beguiling smile, disarmed the most formidable of her adversaries. She regarded the likes of Penn and Dunn as her most worthy challenges.

Ada wanted Gem City to be a wholesome, decent place, a place to live a wholesome, God-fearing life, so she and some of her women friends formed the Gem City Decency and Temperance League of Women Voters. The GCDTLWV was unfortunately, for the women at least, short-lived due to a lack of funding and the lack of a proper meeting place.

Mrs. Nesterud often butted heads with Mr. Penn, which usually ended with him retreating. Nevertheless, Ada was a respected and honored citizen of Gem City. As the years passed, she became an extremely astute politician, winning re-election eight more times for a total of thirty-six years, nine terms on the city council, by the time she threw in the towel.

Joel Penn increased the frequency of his trips to Minneapolis and the length of his stays. He left his trusted saloon manager, Jim Kowalski, in charge of the saloon. Always traveling heavily armed to protect a satchel full of cash he always traveled with, Penn chose to stay at the finest and most luxurious hotels Minneapolis had to offer. He often invited himself to join high-stakes poker games, and had the habit of bringing three or, four sophisticated, well-mannered, brunette—always brunette—prostitutes with him for luck. The women drank, smoked cigarettes, and talked among themselves to help pass the hours while Penn lost hand after hand. He was no match for out of town sharpies from places like New York and Chicago. Penn would quit for the night when his losses ran into the thousands.

One day in July of 1921, he decided to travel to Europe, and wired his bank for more money. He didn't plan on taking any women with him because he was sure to make new friends once he got there.

With the Great War ended, trans-Atlantic voyages had become much safer. His first stop was London, where he enjoyed the nightlife at night, and spent his days at the racetrack. He told himself not to bet on any fat-assed horses and went down to the paddock to make sure he didn't. Some of the fat-assed horses won or placed, anyway. Penn had a good time. He still had plenty of booze on hand and plenty of women so long as he left a trail of money for them to follow.

He next stopped in Monte Carlo to play poker for a while. Then he moved to roulette, where he had the worst luck of his life. The next night, he settled in at a blackjack table and began losing in earnest.

Gambling had never, ever been Penn's strong suit. Suffering heavy losses so often finally took its toll. On New Year's Eve 1922, Penn suddenly stood up, glared at the blackjack dealer, accused him of cheating, slammed down his cards and fell headlong into the table. Word eventually reached Gem City that Joel Penn had died from a heart attack and was buried both physically and financially on the French Riviera in Monaco. He left no heirs.

Meanwhile, Penn's trusted saloon manager, Jim Kowalski, seized the opportunity to have the saloon title transferred to himself. Jim had been embezzling from Penn for years, so he had quite a bit of treasure squirreled away. Seeking a way to make more money, he hired some working girls from Minneapolis to move into Penn's old apartment above the saloon, where they plied their trade.

Things were going pretty well for Jim after Joel Penn died until one of his Minneapolis prostitutes jumped, or was pushed, out of a second story window. Ada Nesterud, well into her third term on the city council had a face-to-face meeting with Kowalski. The remaining prostitutes boarded the next train for Minneapolis. Kowalski moved out of the saloon and left Gem City after asking John Dunn of Dunn Realty to sell the saloon. A man named Michael Flannagan bought the place and he moved his family upstairs into the former bordello that had been Joel Penn's sumptuous apartment.

The Flannagan family, which included Mr. and Mrs. F. and their young children, Tom and Dorothy, ran the saloon until 1936, when Michael Flannagan walked away from selling hooch and went back to farming. The city of Gem City took over the saloon building and turned it into a library. The library was demolished in 1958 after a new one was built a block away.

Tom Flannagan dropped out of high school, hoping to find something more exciting than milking cows. He found excitement not long after the Japanese bombed Pearl Harbor and the United States entered World War Two. Tom was drafted in June 1942 and sent to Fort Riley, Kansas where he learned to drive a tank. He landed in Normandy in September 1944 with a tank named Patsy after his mother. Tom Flannagan drove his tank east with the 9th Armored Division. He helped hold off the Nazis from overrunning Bastogne at the Battle of the Bulge in January 1945, until the 101st Airborne could set up its defense of the city. Tom's unit crossed the Rhine River on the Ludendorff Bridge in March 1945 before the Germans, who had rigged the structure with explosives, could blow it. He was headed into Czechoslovakia on the nineth of May when the war in the European Theater came to an end. Tom returned to Fort Riley, where he met a sweet gal named Eunice. As soon as Tom was discharged, he and Eunice were married. He and his bride returned to Gem City in time for Christmas 1945.

9. Irv Shapiro and the Poteet Family

G em City took possession of a small, wooded area on the old Penn farm through eminent domain for the extension of Main Street. Though the extension was never paved, residents called the city-owned parcel "Penn's Woods" until a real estate developer named Eric Eide purchased the land from the city in 1967. Eide cut down all the trees and platted a new housing development called "Hidden Acres" even though you could plainly see it from the highway. Eide then leveled a grove of pine trees on the east side of town and named it "Whispering Pines". Presumably "Murdered Pines" was already taken.

In the same eminent domain action, the city also took ownership of Joel Penn's ten-acre cemetery and called it "Gethsemane Cemetery". Gem City crafted a new cemetery ordinance that proclaimed there could be no more burials in any of the original churchyard cemeteries. The small Baptist church didn't have to worry about it because they didn't weather the Great Depression and folded up. The remaining parishioners joined a congregation in Cambridge.

Meanwhile, John Dunn, of Dunn Realty, took on a partner, Irv Shapiro. Shapiro brought with him, developers, contractors and architects. The once small and faltering realty firm quickly grew large and prosperous. Dunn and Shapiro was soon the only game in town. A few years later, Irv Shapiro bought out Dunn.

One of Shapiro's investors had expressed interest in the vacant Main Street Baptist Church property, where he planned to build a couple of six-plex apartment buildings. The city paid for the disinterment of the bodies in the church cemetery and moved them, in flatbed trucks, to Gethsemane. Once all the bodies were reinterred, the city held a festive ceremony.

During demolition of the church, just as bulldozers began pushing dirt around in the former cemetery to make room for the foundation of one of the buildings, one of the dozer blades began unearthing shards of wood along with parts of human remains in various stages of decomposition. The pieces were gathered up and placed in hastily built wooden coffins. It didn't matter to Shapiro if the body parts got mixed-up and buried in unmarked graves. Gem City erected a tall, granite obelisk in Gethsemane inscribed with the simple inscription: "Here lies the members of Main Street Baptist Church, 1926-1930."

Then, in a surprise move, Councilwoman Nesterud sued Irv Shapiro for gross negligence in the excavation debacle on the city's behalf. The judge dismissed the case, ruling that Shapiro had "exercised reasonable care and diligence."

There were a few ponds and swamps in Gem City, but only one body of water large enough to be considered a lake. Shapiro and his builders decided to build expensive, lakeshore homes around the dark, murky swimming hole and named it Lake Gem. They cleaned up the lake and stocked it with crappies, sunfish, and small-mouth bass. Bulldozers knocked down a stand of the white birch and willow trees so that the view of the lake was unobstructed.

The building boom continued. Gem City's population reached an all-time peak of 19,800 in 1952. City streets were named after eighteenth and nineteenth century U.S. presidents, except for McKinley, up on the hill, the last street on the eastside. They skipped the second president, John Adams, because Mayor McConnell read someplace that Adams was a mean little prick who didn't deserve to have a street named after him. This probably accounted for the fact that the school kids thought Jefferson was the second president and would consistently get that question wrong on history tests. Gem City avenues were numbered. All streets and avenues started out with two-lanes re-paved, every spring with coal cinders.

There was one street, Van Buren, that started out heading northeast on a diagonal from Main Street, then turning sharply to the north to avoid cutting through the Poteet farm.

There were many townsfolk who didn't care if the street ran right through Poteet's house. The Poteets were the orneriest, meanest, homeliest family to ever set foot in Gem City, the state, and perhaps the planet. Mr. and Mrs. Poteet, their three boys and two girls, were somewhat, let's say, sociopathic. It seemed to be their nature.

One early spring evening, during a sleet storm, when the rain drops turn into crystalline needles, old man and old lady Poteet were busy tying one on at Flannagan's when someone came running into the saloon yelling about the weird, rosy glow in the eastern sky. It was time for the Poteets to go home, anyway. So, they headed in that direction to investigate the phenomenon. When they got home, they discovered that their kids, overcome with boredom, had set the barn on fire—just for fun. The sleet storm had come along and put out the fire, but half the barn had already burned to the ground.

No one helped Poteet rebuild his barn, because the entire family would curse people just for looking at them—not that anybody looked at them for more than a couple of minutes.

It was rumored that Mr. Poteet had done some hard time at Stillwater Prison for trying to kill a man with a pitchfork. Some say it was Mrs. Poteet who did time for trying to kill a man with a pitchfork. Be that as it may, they were very bad people who did very bad things.

By the time their kids were spread out across grades in elementary school, they had all been expelled for conspiring to murder their teachers. And since they all carried knives, anything was possible. Mix criminality with ignorance and the proclivity toward violence, you get the Poteets.

The following June, a monster tornado happened to choose the Poteet farm. The twister touched down, destroying animals, buildings and people, all eight of them—the middle-aged and the teen-aged, before they could make it to the cellar. Shapiro subdivided the devastated, treeless land and built six new homes.

On the point of land at the intersection of Main and Van Buren, Colonel Jack Parks, his wife Amanda, and their young son, made their home. After a time, Jack and Amanda would add three more sons.

10. The Illustrious Colonel Parks

C olonel Parks' story was embellished and escalated to mythic proportions over time by his friends, neighbors and townsfolk. He neither refuted, nor corrected any of the stories, having fueled some of them himself. Though Parks became somewhat of a legend, the truth, as it always is, was a little bit plainer.

Jack Parks grew up in rural western Pennsylvania, migrated to Minnesota to go to the University of Minnesota's Agricultural school, but chose architecture instead. The summer before his senior year, he returned home to Pennsylvania for a visit.

His father, Alvin Parks, a former Corporal in the Union's Grand Army of the Republic, took the younger Parks with him to the cemetery at Gettysburg, where Civil War veterans from both sides gathered with their families to commemorate the twenty-fifth anniversary of the Battle of Gettysburg. Parks blinked away tears when he saw the veterans, some of whom wore their uniforms, complete with medals around their necks or pinned on their chests. A number of them were missing arms and legs, but they swaggered the best they could and marched in an impromptu parade. Parks' father also marched, in his blue uniform with the yellow striped chevrons of his corporal rank and red stripes down the legs of his trousers.

Alvin told Jack that the Civil War, as horrible as any war in history, had produced some of the finest, bravest, God-fearing soldiers that there ever were—Yanks as well as Rebs.

Jack Parks returned to the University of Minnesota that fall and graduated the following spring. He remembered the lessons his father had impressed upon him with regard to service to one's country. In 1891, right after graduation, Jack enlisted in the Army Corps of Engineers. He reported to Fort Snelling for training and received his commission as a Second Lieutenant.

While stationed in Galveston in 1898, he heard the news that Spain had sunk the U.S.S. Maine, and that war had been declared. By then, he had attained the rank of Major and fully expected to go to Havana but was sent to Manila instead.

After only a few months in the Philippines, Major Parks

contracted malaria and spent the rest of the war in an army hospital. Following the war, he rose to the rank of Lieutenant Colonel. Near the end of his career, Jack Parks became a full bird Colonel.

Ready to settle down to civilian life, Colonel Parks was discharged in 1906. He returned to Pennsylvania, where he met and married his wife Amanda and started a family. The only work in Pennsylvania at that time was farming, working in the coal mines or, the steel mills. Jack had other plans, despite the objections of his parents and in-laws.

While in the army, Jack had met a couple of enlisted men from St. Stephen Point, Minnesota. They made the place sound like a paradise, a new frontier, a good place to raise a family. So, about seven months after Jack Jr. was born, the Colonel and Mrs. Parks packed up and took the train to St. Stephen Point. He never again saw or heard from the two enlisted men who'd painted such an attractive picture of his new hometown.

The Colonel and Amanda made their home on the triangular lot on the southeast side of Main Street where Van Buren Street intersected. For a while, Jack thought that St. Stephen Point had been named after his pointed piece of property.

On the north end of the property, the wider part, he designed and built a two-story white house with an open wrap-around porch. They had a small vegetable garden and built a stable near one side of the house for their six riding horses and a garage for Jack's Ford. The retired Army colonel became a gentleman farmer—more gentleman, than farmer.

If local folks, grownups and kids, wanted to go horseback riding, Jack would take them on trail rides around his property. This probably started the rumor that Jack had been in the cavalry. Everyone asked him if he'd ever met Teddy Roosevelt or any of his Rough Riders, which pissed-off Jack. He considered T.R. nothing more than an overrated blowhard, an undeserving hero whose reputation was exaggerated at best. When asked, the Colonel would compose himself and replied that he had never met Teddy because he was stationed in the Philippines to quell an insurrection.

"Teddy, you see, was in Puerto Rico, running up and down hills," Colonel Parks explained.

Amanda quickly gave birth to three more sons in the Colonel's house, and each time a midwife came over to help with the delivery.

Each time a son was born, Jack would throw a huge party. He invited just about everybody in town on those occasions. He always had plenty of brandy and cigars on hand. The Victrola was moved to a window by the porch, and Sousa marches were played, along with a few Enrico Caruso records. House guests would always sit in rows of rattan rocking chairs on the porch drinking, smoking and listened to the recordings.

Mr. and Mrs. Erroll Nesterud, the Mayor and the rest of the village council became frequent party guests at the Parks' home. Joel Penn stopped by occasionally. Ada Nesterud, contrary to popular opinion, did not fit the stereotype of the axe-wielding, anti-barleycorn, temperance woman. Ada crusaded against married men staying out half the night drinking and whoring.

At the Colonel's parties, when the group of guests weren't solving the world's problems, Parks, a tall, thin, straight-backed man, regaled his guests with tales of the Spanish-American War and how he and his outfit once put-down a large-scale Filipino riot.

Since no one living in St. Stephen County had been in the Civil War, or any other war for that matter, Colonel Parks became the county's first war hero and was celebrated in St. Stephen Point.

Even when there were no house guests, Parks would sit in a rocker on the south side of the porch to, watch the occasional automobile pass by on Main or Van Buren, drinking his customary three snifters of brandy, smoking a cigar, listening to Caruso. After that, he retired for the night.

Parks played the stock market to supplement his army pension, so he made frequent trips in his Ford to Minneapolis, spending the night in downtown Minneapolis and returning the following day. Amanda didn't mind at all because Jack was making a ton of money.

One day, the Colonel and Amanda showed up at St. Stephens Point Town Hall to present city leaders an ambitious plan. Jack had designed a war memorial replete with flowers, shrubbery and two marble monuments, one for the Civil War and one for the Spanish-American War. He explained that he would donate the extreme point of his property if the town paid for the monuments. The council agreed, and Jack informed them that he would invite veterans of both wars to attend a big dedication ceremony when the monuments were completed.

"I shall be the master of ceremonies."

Everyone loved the idea. The Mayor, members of the council and a few leading citizens could give speeches. Of course, they would need a military-type brass band, and were forced to hire a band from out of town.

Parks invited his father and some of his father's old cronies from the Civil War. He also invited some of his army pals to attend the festivities. A small coincidence indeed, no one invited had held the rank of Colonel or above.

Dedication of the memorial was scheduled to take place on the Fourth of July. Joel Penn arrived in his car ahead of a truck loaded with whiskey and beer from his saloon, and food enough for an army of picnickers. Attendees brought benches and chairs to sit on, while others sat on the grass. There were fireworks and sincere, pedantic speeches, including a recitation of Lincoln's Gettysburg Address by members of Miss Schmidt's sixth-grade class. The band played Sousa, and the Veterans marched.

Colonel Parks stood between the monuments wearing his full-dress olive drab uniform, his campaign hat jauntily cocked to one side, to review the troops. The only thing different from his Army days was that he had trimmed the handlebars from his thick, black mustache. His medals gleaming, he held a riding crop under his arm. He also wore jodhpurs and knee-high, spit-shined brown boots and of course, his eagle insignias. This too, furthered the false, but highly intentional impression that Colonel Parks had commanded a cavalry unit during the Spanish American War.

A few years later, there were rumblings of war in Europe. President Wilson volunteered a half-million troops to aid Britain and France in the First World War. A few men from St. Stephen Point volunteered, including Colonel Parks' sons. Three of them enlisted in the Army; Jack Jr. joined the Marines. On the eleventh day of the eleventh month at the eleventh hour in 1918, peace broke out. The Colonel's boys who'd joined the Army came home without a scratch; Jack Jr. was killed in France and was laid to rest in a French cemetery. Erroll Nesterud never returned either; he got laid in a Paris brothel.

The town erected another marble monument to the War Memorial Point with Jack Jr.'s name inscribed in the marble. The WWI monument was dedicated in December, and each successive year, a somber ceremony was held on Armistice Day instead of July

Fourth. Some of the town's World War veterans and a dwindling number from the Civil War attended—this time, minus Alvin Parks, who had died the previous year.

Even though the name was changed to Veterans' Day following World War Two, some of the old-timers continued to commemorate Armistice Day on the Eleventh of November.

11. Baseball comes to Gem City

Gem City was growing again. More homes were being built while large, family-owned farms were shrinking. The old blacksmith's shop on the edge of town grew into a gigantic foundry, employing hundreds of men. The munitions plant, which was so vital during the wars, was scaled back to meet the needs of sportsmen. Grain elevators serving the remaining farms continued to expand along the railroad tracks—some standing taller than the cliff on the other side of the river. Limestone from the cliff was quarried, cut into blocks and was used to build public and commercial buildings in Gem City.

Colonel Parks was hired as the architect for most of the buildings in the business district along Main Street, which was now teeming with activity day and night. The Ruby Theater, built in 1926, showed silent films and presented live stage performances. Gem City rivaled the City of St. Stephen, not only in population, but as a successful metropolis. Main Street became the first and, for a while, the only street in either city paved with asphalt.

Councilwoman Ada Nesterud and a contingent of her friends, once paid a visit to Colonel Parks and asked him to run for mayor, assuring him that he would most certainly be elected. Parks declined, saying that he would be uncomfortable being in the public eye.

At a time when the game of baseball had become increasingly popular as the nation's pastime thanks to Babe Ruth, an idea struck Parks—an epiphany, he called it—and he formally presented it to Mrs. Nesterud and the rest of the city council.

Colonel Jack and Amanda, arrived at one of the buildings Jack had designed, Gem City City Hall. Ada Nesterud silenced the chatter of the other four councilmembers.

"We were just about to begin," she said. "you have the floor, Colonel."

Jack cleared his throat and began. "There's a large, swampy area just south of First Avenue. I propose filling that lot with sand and black dirt and turning it into a baseball field."

"Baseball?" intoned the mayor. "That sport is only popular out east. Who'd play it here in Gem City?"

Mrs. Nesterud was the one who really ran City Hall. Nesterud knew it, Parks knew it, and everyone else in town knew it too. Ada, her hands folded on top of the long, white pine table that served as the council dais, raised her left eyebrow, scanned the rest of the councilmen and said, "It is clearly Colonel Parks' intention to bring culture to this city, and baseball is a very cultured sport. I hadn't thought much of it until I visited Chicago and saw the Bambino himself play. I am convinced that baseball will catch on right here in Gem City."

"And if we do go ahead and build it," said the mayor, looking directly at Parks, "after whom do you suppose we name it? You?"

The Colonel's face reddened. His voice rose an octave above normal conversational tone. "That's ridiculous! What the hell do you take me for?"

Just as Jack spoke those words, he noticed that all eyes were focused on Amanda, who stood beside her husband with fingertips over her mouth in an attempt to stifle a laugh.

When Jack looked at her, she coughed self-consciously and said, "Excuse me, Jack, please continue."

"There's nothing more to say," Jack bellowed. "So vote on it then."

Without further discussion, the council voted in favor of building a ballpark. Construction began without delay, and Gem City caught baseball fever. Baseball became the only sport of major interest, and not just April through September, but year round.

The high school had a mediocre football team, but that didn't matter because they formed a pretty good baseball team. The high school baseball coach told his players that they weren't allowed to play any other sport in school—only baseball. During the winter months, they practiced in the school gymnasium.

Some of the farmers and merchants formed the city baseball team. The foundry and the munitions plant had teams, too. Other towns had teams, as well—towns like Cambridge, Princeton, Brainerd, St. Stephen and Anoka. Since there weren't enough town teams to play each other, so the industrial teams were also included in the league.

The Gem City Diamonds would often play the munitions plant and the foundry despite the suspicion that the foundry employed ringers. It mattered little because the thick-necked, stocky farmers played as if the lives depended on winning. Fans couldn't stop talking about Ox Brewster's line-shot homer to center that put a hole right through the scoreboard. All of Gem City's teams were excellent. So good were they that the famed Minneapolis Millers were invited up to play an exhibition game with the Diamonds, however, the Millers never responded.

Colonel Parks was a ubiquitous presence at every town celebration and parade. In Fourth of July, Armistice Day, or Columbus Day parades, Jack always led the procession astride one of his horses. The horse would bow, nod, dance and prance. The parade-goers loved it when Jack made his horse rear-up on its hind legs and wave to the audience with its front hooves.

At the start of every baseball season, Colonel Parks volunteered to throw out the first pitch. He didn't have to be asked. Every year the crowd roared with approval. Jack wore his familiar Army uniform. He would remove his hat, carefully placing it beside the pitcher's mound, before delivering the pitch.

The Colonel tried to get his sons to play for the Diamonds, but they had other plans; two of them got married in Parks' front yard. The youngest never married. He earned a Ph.D. in English Literature and became a professor at a small college in Nebraska. The other two sons moved away from Gem City as soon as they finished high school.

Jack and Amanda ended up living alone in their lonely square house. He found himself barely content with the fact that he had brought baseball to Gem City, had helped John Dunn develop half the town, and had amassed more riches than any man to set foot in Gem City. The Colonel's wealth even surpassed that of Joel Penn, if only by a few hundred-thousand dollars.

12. Colonel Parks and The Crash

Colonel Parks' stock analyst phoned him with unimaginable news on October 29, 1929, which history remembers as The Crash—the event that ignited the Great Depression. Jack jumped into his new Model T. Amanda tried to run after him, but he was already roaring down the driveway. He drove, only stopping for gas, all the way to Minneapolis to see his panicky advisor.

Later that day, as witnesses later recalled, a tall, thin man, appearing drunk, got out of his car and walked in front of a streetcar on Marquette Avenue, standing defiantly on the tracks with his hands on his hips.

The Colonel's funeral was a monumental event in Gem City. St. Stephen Lutheran Church was packed with both the powerful and the weak, all paying homage to one of the town's most noble citizens. Only one aging Civil War veteran made it to the ceremony.

Ada Nesterud took to the pulpit and delivered the first eulogy. "A mighty warrior has fallen," she proclaimed. "We will remember Colonel Parks as a kind and gifted man, strong yet compassionate."

Reverend Webster shifted nervously in his wooden, straight-backed chair next to the wall beside the pulpit. Colonel Parks' death was a suicide and the church didn't condone that sort of thing. But, at the soulful urging and pleading of Widow Parks, the Reverend acquiesced.

"Magnificent, though he was." Ada stopped, tears in her eyes; her lower lip started to quiver. She couldn't continue and stepped away from the pulpit. Murmurs rose up and swept through the church, from the front pews to the back. "Mrs. Nesterud, of all people, can't go through with it," the people whispered.

Widow Parks, sitting beside her sons, looked over at Mayor Nelson as he struggled to his feet. Scheduled to be the next speaker, the Mayor decided it was time to rescue Nesterud. A stout, balding man whose black suit, as well as his shoes, were a size too small, the Mayor had a problem walking. For every two steps forward, he took one step back. "

Drunk again. Murmurs rose once more as he made his way to the pulpit, taking tiny steps, his arms stretched out on either side like a tightrope walker. Felix paused to touch the Colonel's flag-draped coffin, steadied himself and caught his breath. He looked around for Nesterud, but she had already passed him going the other way and returned to her seat beside Felix's wife, Elsie, who sat there, her head down, embarrassed.

The Mayor took some notes from his pocket and fumbled for his reading glasses. "Must've left 'em in my other suit." His chuckle echoed through the silently attentive congregation. He squinted briefly at his notes, then put them aside.

"My friends, I want to tell you about Colonel Parks, but first, let me share a conversation he and I had only two weeks ago after I had written a letter to that filthy swine, Andrew J. Volstead, regarding the immoral Eighteenth Amendment we've all come to know as Prohibition.

"Well, in the letter, I invited Volstead and his underlings to Gem City knowing that our illustrious Police Department, led by me of course, would warn our citizens to hide their hooch. That way, Andy Volstead would see that we were obeying the law and henceforth leave us alone. The Colonel, here," Felix pointed at the casket, "told me not to send my letter. 'Ok,' I replied, 'I'm not gonna send it, but if Volstead ever shows up in this town, I'll just hafta shoot him!'"

Nelson felt a tap on his shoulder. Reverend Webster said softly, "Thank you, Mr. Mayor, for your kind words. I know the Colonel's family appreciates your remarks today. You may have a seat, now."

Oh, you're gonna get it, Felix, thought Elsie Nelson. The corners of her mouth turned upward and broke into a smile ... *just when you least expect it.*

Colonel Jack Parks was interred with full military honors in Gethsemane Cemetery where a gray granite obelisk would soon be erected. Mayor Nelson presented Widow Parks with the three-cornered flag. She gave the flag back to the city and asked John Dunn to sell the house. Amanda Parks, who quickly grew tired of being referred to as Widow Parks, moved back to Philadelphia and married a dentist. Dunn bought the house himself for a generous discount. Perhaps one of the first in her generation to hyphenate her last name, Amanda became known as Mrs. Amanda Levinsky-Parks, wife of Dr. Al Levinsky, D.D.S.

13. Madame Tereshkova

I n 1928, Ada Nesterud and friends marched to third and Madison to picket the house of fortune teller, Madame Tereshkova. About twenty married men, through coerced confessions, admitted that they had visited Tereshkova's residence, but not for the purpose of having their fortunes told.

Marie Tereshkova, a dark, mysterious and attractive Romanian woman in her late forties, emigrated to Gem City after being chased out of New York City by the police. She bought a large house from Dunn and Shapiro, and, by day, read palms, tea leaves and told fortunes in her parlor; by night, she removed her babushka to become one of Gem City's most successful employers. The prostitutes she employed were not allowed downstairs until after five p.m. Then, working girls of all shapes and sizes, would come downstairs to meet and greet the clientele. The customers sat in Madame's parlor, transformed from a dimly lighted fortune-telling room into a dimly lighted waiting room. They tried to relax in overstuffed chairs and love seats, nervously sipping whiskey and puffing cigars until a woman appeared in the doorway and signaled one of them that is was his turn. The women thought it uproariously funny when they announced their customers by their titles: judge, councilman, mayor, chief, colonel, professor, etcetera. At first, the men were uncomfortably embarrassed, but because they all knew each other, and they too would belt out raspy laughs and slap their knees. It was a lot of fun.

It was fun, until Mrs. Nesterud showed up. Nesterud and her gang caused quite a stir out in front of the brothel, so much of a stir that Madame Tereshkova phoned the police. Captain Henderson and Sergeant Sullivan were dispatched to quell the disturbance. The policemen threatened to arrest Nesterud and her accomplices and began confiscating the picket signs reading: "Whores live here," and "Our husbands are visiting whores." Nesterud informed Henderson that they had a constitutional right to peacefully assemble. Sullivan, then spoke up to say that they only had the right to assemble for religious purposes. The First Amendment was loudly brought up and so the argument escalated until the police chief was summoned, which led to the discovery that the Chief was inside the house at the time and had been there for a least a couple of hours. The next day, Councilwoman Nesterud had the county sheriff raid the place and shut it down.

The county district court judge was ordered to preside over Tereshkova's deportation hearing. He had decided to go easy on her if she provided a confidential list of names of her most regular customers. When the judge saw his own name listed, he signed the deportation papers and sent the Madame back to Romania. In his chambers, the judge touched a match to the list.

A new saying was making the rounds: "You can fight City Hall, but you can't fight Ada Nesterud!"

Ada had many more fights to win and lose while on the city council. Ada opposed plans for a new state highway unveiled in 1939. She explained that she had calculated it would only save twenty minutes of driving time to Minneapolis, as opposed to taking Main Street and linking up to the county road, something people had done for decades. She lost that fight and the W.P.A. started working on the two-lane project.

The new state highway headed south through the middle of St. Stephen County and hooked west when it came to Gem City. Main Street came up to meet it as it continued west to the railroad tracks, where it veered southward again.

Ada demanded that a stop sign, at least, be placed at the end of Main Street to make people stop and look before turning onto the highway. Nesterud would finally get her way, when the first traffic fatality occurred at that intersection.

A car carrying a man and a woman had casually turned onto the highway, when they were struck from behind by a truck loaded with construction materials. A stop sign was put up on the end of Main Street and "slow" signs were placed, one for each direction, on the highway.

As always, Ada Nesterud continued to be the conscience of the community: the city's watchdog whenever the City Fathers leapt headlong into a project without any consideration to foresight.

Shortly after the death of Colonel Parks, a city councilmember once made a motion to name the baseball park "Parks Park". Mrs. Nesterud slapped the palms of her hands down on the table, rolled her eyes and snarled, "I've never heard of anything so goddam stupid in my life!" She then calmly suggested the name, "Parks Field".

She continued to be re-elected when others, mayors and city councilmembers, were not.

Another fatality occurred at the Main Street, state highway intersection in 1957. Ada had the state government put up semaphore signals and a streetlight at the intersection. Once that was done, she retired from politics in spite of protests from her friends, which by that time, were many.

Later that year, a retirement banquet was held in her honor at the high school cafeteria. After four glasses of cheap champagne, Ada got up to give her final public speech. She smiled her most pleasant smile and cheerfully began, directing her remarks to the city councilmembers who were in attendance:

"I now pass the torch to a new generation of imbeciles. I beg you, all of you, please don't screw things up."

A few people tittered, thinking that she was only being facetious, but then, they too, slumped back in stunned silence when they realized she wasn't. "Of course, it's the champagne talking," some whispered. Ada stopped smiling and sternly warned the city council that they must plan for future generations, and to be of service to the entire community, not just to themselves. She made a few new friends that night but retained a few old enemies.

When Ada Nesterud died in 1961, everyone in the county knew of her passing. Lights on Main Street were dimmed in her honor. After a long funeral procession, which traveled the entire length of Main Street, she was buried at Gethsemane, per her request, at six a.m. on a Monday morning. The sun had begun to rise and one could see, even from the cemetery, the flag on the rooftop at city hall being raised briskly to the top of the twenty-four foot staff, then lowered slowly to half-mast.

In accordance with her last will and testament, she was buried next to her friend, Colonel Jack Parks; all of her worldly possessions were liquidated and dispersed to Gem City government departments to be used for city improvement.

Mrs. Nesterud will always be remembered as the city's watchdog.

She had an orange tomcat named Mark who, until the first snowstorm in November, used to curl up and sleep on her grave. After the storm, Mark was never seen again.

Ada would also be forever and fondly remembered as a liberal skeptic.

14. Scandal!

Ben Wilkinson was a big-boned, homely, flatulent man. He was also the town drunk. His heavy-drinking wife Tess was a big-boned, flatulent, homely woman. The two of them together could change the atmosphere of any social gathering—in more ways than one.

They had two daughters. Their eldest daughter's name was Ada, who later became known as Mrs. Erroll Nesterud. Her parents didn't have to worry much about her. They did, however, worry a great deal about their youngest daughter, Inez.

Inez didn't look like the rest of the Wilkersons, with her dark hair and dark complexion, but she was short and stocky like the rest of them. She matured early and by her junior year in high school, she looked like a full-grown woman. So, in the fall of 1921, she decided that some of her male classmates should become as mature as she.

Each day at lunchtime she would choose a boy and they would take an old, wool blanket and got out behind the school, past the student outhouse and spread the blanket behind the trunks of a couple of huge oak trees. Inez'd lie on her back, coyly spread her knees with her fingertips and lift her dress high enough to expose her large, firm breasts. Her nipples were large and dark. On those days, she wouldn't wear her bloomers.

With some of the virgin boys, all it would take is one look at her dark, musty, pubic hair triangle and they would ejaculate in their pants. She preferred, in fact, that they not ejaculate inside of her. Inez would either look away, or close her sad, brown eyes when they lay, spent, on top of her. She had a couple of rules. One: she'd do one boy per day. Two: the boys had to forever swear discretion, no matter what.

Inez wasn't a very good student. She got "D" in most subjects. Quite suddenly, she got an "A" in Geography and yet another "A" in Math. This could've been attributed to the fact that she had seduced the male teachers of her worst subjects. The following year, she graduated as valedictorian.

Somehow, the scandal leaked out and Inez was put on a train to Minneapolis. She landed a job at the Washburn-Crosby flour mill and worked there for about a year, until she met a nice young pharmacist by the name of Alan Goetz. After they were married, the pharmacist built her a little three-bedroom bungalow in Northeast Minneapolis.

After Inez left town, her respectable sister Ada stopped telling people that she even had a sister. A few years later, Inez was savaged by an aggressive type of cancer which affected all of her internal organs. Her pharmacist husband Alan procured morphine for his young wife and gave her daily injections to help ease her pain. At the end, he kissed her on the forehead, gave her a triple dose and tearfully said "Goodbye.".

Ben and Tess Wilkerson went to their graves without knowing that Inez had been happily married and gave birth to two sons.

15. Mayor Nelson, Elroy and Elsie

Following Jack Parks' funeral, Mayor Nelson spoke his mind regarding the Colonel. "I've never met a man who could blow his own horn like Jack did."

"You shouldn't speak ill of the dead, Felix," Elsie admonished her husband, "he's hardly cold in the ground."

"Oh, I know, but his war's been over for thirty years, for God's sake, and he still talked about it like it was yesterday. He never even mentioned Jack Jr., anymore. Now, there was a real hero, if you ask me."

"And Colonel Parks wasn't a hero?"

"Yeah—I mean no. It's just that I'm fed up with hearing about the Colonel. The Colonel this and the Colonel that. Him and his girlfriend. Two of a kind. And you know damn well who I mean. Ada Nesterud, is just a cigar smoking, brandy swilling Bolshevik! She's two-faced, too. All the time spouting this temperance bullshit. But she drinks like a fish—probably more than me."

"Felix, nobody drinks more than you and besides, how do you know she was the Colonel's girlfriend?"

"Beause at the Colonel's parties, she was always the last one to leave; his wife put the kids to bed and went to bed, herself. And there sat Ada and Colonel Parks alone on the porch, drunk, making goo-goo eyes at each other."

"I'm sure it's just your stupid imagination. And why, of all times and places, did you have to get drunk before giving that eulogy?"

"What the hell are you talkin' about? It's not our church and it wasn't even Sunday!"

"Besides that, Felix, did you have to bring up Volstead and that dumb letter? Didn't you see people looking at you? And what did that have to do with Jack Parks?"

"You think you're so smart! I mentioned it because Congressman Andy Volstead betrayed his own constituency, right here in Minnesota, and everybody knows it. It's stupid to take away something that's legal and can be taxed. That's gonna be my platform for re-election. Repeal the Eighteenth! So, what do ya think now?"

"You don't wanna know what I'm thinking."

On a blustery, cold, rainy November day, Elsie Nelson planned a clandestine meeting with Elroy Gibbons at noon in a secluded area of Penn's Woods. Elsie lived close and opted to walk over. Elroy closed his store for lunch and drove his old Chevrolet. Elsie climbed into his car.

"Does Felix know you're pregnant?"

"Yeah, and the old goat is overjoyed. He thinks it'll get him re-elected because it proves his manliness."

"Listen, Els, let's get to the point. Did he make you pregnant, or did I?"

"I don't know. I'm so confused. We haven't had relations in twenty years. Well, at least ten. I was always sure that he was impudent."

Elroy was sure she meant impotent but didn't correct her because Felix could be both. Elroy was saying something, but Elsie wasn't listening. She lit a cigarette and gazed out the window at the misty rain.

Could Felix have really done it? She tried to remember if there were any breaks in what became her nightly routine: turning off the damn radio, taking Felix's shoes off as he lay asleep on the couch, and putting the lid back on the half empty fruit jar containing clear ethyl alcohol. He never told anyone where he got it.

"Well, how far along are you?" asked Elroy.

Elsie turned back to the conversation. "I missed my cycle last month."

"There you go. It wasn't me. We stopped fooling around when you thought Felix was getting suspicious. That was more than two months ago."

"God, Elroy, I don't know what to do. I think constantly about divorcing him and I want to keep this baby, but if you're not the father … "

"Look, Els, if you want to divorce him, wait till after the baby's born."

"But it'll probably ruin his chances for re-election."

"What do you care about his goddam election?"

"Elroy, if I divorce Felix, will you leave your wife and marry me?"

"I don't know, I mean, maybe. We'll have to wait and see. I love my wife and kids. I don't know."

In the weeks and months that followed, Elsie Nelson's fears regarding the probability of Elroy Gibbons effectuating indiscreet remarks about their illicit relationship were suddenly relieved of any consequence. Her fears were allayed when the bank foreclosed on his haberdashery. Unfortunately for Elroy, he had packaged his mortgage to include both his store and his residence above the store. It was rumored that he and his family were headed to Sonoma, California, to pick grapes.

On a hot, steamy evening in July, the mercury still hovering at eighty-eight degrees, Elsie took the Nash and drove herself thirty miles to the county hospital in St. Stephen. Her husband, Felix, was drinking more heavily and couldn't drive anymore. This being her third child, Elsie had a relatively easy delivery. Elsie named her daughter, Stella Marie Nelson. Now, there was no doubt in her mind that Felix was Stella's father. She looked just like him: short, fat and bald.

Mayor Felix Nelson was getting ready to preside over the regular bi-monthly city council meeting one Monday evening in August.

"Elsie, where the hell is my blue tie!?"

"Will you shuddup, you'll wake the baby!"

Felix stormed out of the bathroom and swung a roundhouse right at Elsie's head, but missed. A left-cross caught her on the cheekbone and sent her reeling toward the couch, where she slumped, dazed, silver dots dancing in front of her eyes.

"Now, I suppose I gotta walk over there!" Felix bellowed as he stomped out, tieless; behind him, the screen door slapped shut.

Elsie took an icepick, chopped some ice for a cold compress and gingerly held it to her eye. "Thank God, he didn't wake the baby," she whispered aloud.

She tuned the radio to CBS and commentator, H.V. Kaltenborn while she waited for Felix to return. The telephone rang—Elsie answered it quickly.

"Mrs. Nelson? Sorry to bother you, this is the council secretary, Mrs. Chalmers. Elsie, it's Felix."

"What's he done, now?"

"Well, he was drunk and yelling bad things about Congressman Volstead, saying that he was going to hunt Volstead down and kill him, that if he couldn't find him in Goodhue County, he'd find him in Washington. Then he threw up in a wire wastebasket, and if that wasn't bad enough, he threw up on the council table and slumped headlong into his own vomit. Elsie, I mean to tell you that this is a public meeting and we just can't have that kind of behavior. So, I'm having a policeman bring him home."

"Thanks, Alice, I'll be waiting. Tell the officer not to knock or ring the bell."

A while later, Elsie looked out the front door to watch a policeman help Felix out of the patrol car and slowly guide him up the long sidewalk.

"Evening, Mrs. Nelson," the officer grunted, struggling to walk the Mayor forward.

"Shhh," Elsie whispered, "baby's asleep."

"I don't think that kid's even mine," slurred Felix.

Elsie dropped her icepack to help get Felix into the house.

"What on earth happened to your eye, ma'am?" She forced a tiny laugh and explained that the baby had accidentally kicked her. "Those things happen, I guess. Here's the mayor's suitcoat. You're gonna hafta have it dry cleaned. It's covered in vomit."

"Thank you, Officer … "

" … Schmidt, ma'am. Gerald Schmidt. If you'll pardon me for asking, ma'am, where does the Mayor get his liquor?"

"I don't know, Gerald Schmidt, no one does."

Officer Schmidt returned to his beat.

"Oh, good," Felix turned toward the radio, "Kaltenborn's on."

Elsie snapped off the radio. "No time for that, Felix. You just get undressed and I'll draw you a nice, warm bath."

"Okay, thanks. By the way, I'm so sorry I hit you. It won't happen again."

No it won't! It won't ever happen again!

Felix was lying back in the water like a beached walrus, sipping liquor from his fruit jar when Elsie entered the bathroom.

"Feeling any better?" she asked with a look of mock concern.

"Yeah, could you get me a little piece of ice for my drink?"

Elsie went to the kitchen and got an icepick. She found it surprisingly easy to control the rage that was building inside of her, but it was building, nonetheless. As she frenetically chopped the ice into tiny bits, she wondered if the iceman was Felix's bootlegger. He held out the jar and poured the ice chips into it.

Inexplicably, from Felix's viewpoint, Elsie snatched a towel from the rack and began soaking it in the bathtub. "What do ya think yer doin'?" He croaked.

"Just relax," she cooed, "I remembered that this towel's dirty. I'll get you a clean one." She doubled the soaked towel over, then twisted it around and around till it looked like a heavy rope. *God,* she thought, *it must weigh at least twelve pounds!*

Elsie felt her heart pounding faster and faster. A voice, a command hallucination, screamed, *Now! Do it now!* Felix suddenly sat up. The voice shouted to Elsie, *Perfect! Do it now!* Elsie hoisted the towel and hit Felix in the side of the head. His head bounced off the ceramic-tiled wall. He started yelling. The baby woke and started crying. The voice shrieked, *Do it again!* She hit him in the forehead. His head snapped back. Even the voice lost control. Elsie took over screaming. With each syllable of her epithets, she swung the heavy towel down on his head and each time, his head hit the wall.

"You dir-ty, rot-ten, son-uva-bitch! You no-good, rot-ten, fat, bast-ard! This one is for my black eye and this one is for Stel-la Ma-rie, you stink-ing, piece of shit!"

Well, that certainly didn't take long, Elsie mused as Felix slid below the water's roiled surface. Small, scarlet bubbles came from his nostrils. Then nothing. Elsie cocked her head to one side and remarked, cheerfully, "Gem City giveth and Gem City taketh away."

Felix's eyes were wide open in terror, but he was dead—at last. There wasn't a mark on him, except for the bump on the side of his head where it had hit the wall. In fact, it looked exactly like he had a heart attack and drowned in the tub, which happened all the time.

Stella Marie was wailing in the bedroom. "It's all right, Stella Marie darling. Momma will make things all better. I promise."

16. After Felix Nelson

Less than two weeks after Mayor Nelson's burial, the city council began planning for the 1930 election. The top mayoral candidate that November was councilman Joseph Beemish. Most were certain that Beemish would accept nomination and equally certain he would win. The only question before the council was, whom should they ask to serve as interim Mayor to fill the remaining three months of Felix Nelson's term?

Councilwoman Ada Nesterud was leafing through the city charter when she discovered an ordinance that read: "In the event the Mayor, or member of the city council dies, or is otherwise incapacitated, thereby failing to complete his elected term, then the official's spouse shall succeed him if he/she so desires. If the aforementioned public official is unmarried, then his closest relative residing within the corporate boundaries of Gem City shall succeed him if he/she so desires."

Nesterud phoned Elsie Nelson and explained the situation, meeting at first some reticence from Elsie and then a fair amount of resistance. "Ada, this is gonna be a lotta work. Who am I gonna get to take care of my baby?"

"Well, there's Mrs. Dunn."

"The real estate man's wife? Not on your life!"

"Okay then. How about old Mrs. Thompson? She's raised seven of her own and almost twice as many grandchildren."

"All right, you can come over next Tuesday and we'll talk about it."

Nesterud, a district court judge, a photographer from the *Bugle* and the three other councilmembers descended on Elsie's two-bedroom bungalow along with a copy of the city charter.

"Who's the joker with the camera?" Elsie asked.

"Oh, he's just from the *Bugle*. Your picture's going to be in the paper."

"Okay, let's get this over with, then. My baby's been colicky all day and now that I finally got her to sleep."

"This won't take long, dear. I just want to tell you how wonderful you look!"

"Thank you, Ada. I gained thirty pounds during the pregnancy and only lost five pounds after Stella was born."

"Well, that's good, Elsie. You were always such a thin girl. The extra pounds make you look younger and healthier."

Ada noticed the men sighing heavily and awkwardly looking around.

"Okay, then. Getting down to business," Ada began. "It says in the charter that you can succeed Felix as interim mayor. You know, to continue his work."

"And what the hell work are you talkin' about?" Elsie chimed in. "What work did he ever do?"

Ada glanced nervously at the councilmen. "Anyway, we need you to accept the position until November and another four months until the inauguration in March."

"Okay, I'll do it just this once. I have a child to raise and that's more important than this foolishness."

Judge Manning brought his own Bible for the solemn swearing-in ceremony. Everyone almost laughed when he came to the part in the oath when he asked Elsie "to defend Gem City against all enemies, foreign and domestic." It was done. Gem City had a new Mayor.

The men left Mayor Elsie's house, but Mrs. Nesterud lingered to talk to Elsie.

"Ada, is this stuff, being Mayor and everything, gonna take a lot of time away from my baby? It seems that Felix was working all the time at City Hall."

"What? Are you joking? Felix hardly spent any time at City Hall. Sure, he would make it to the meetings every other Monday, but that's about it."

"That sonuva bitch! Here I was givin' him a ride to work every single day! Where the hell was he?"

"I hate to tell you this, dear, but I think he was at Madame Tereshkova's house most of the time."

"You mean, the whorehouse?"

"Yes. You don't mince words and that's what I admire most about you."

In late October 1930, Gem City Mayor Pro Tem, Elsie Nelson was quoted in the *Bugle* as saying, "If nominated, I will not run, if elected, I will not serve."

Readers of the *Bugle* immediately recognized the quote as one belonging to President Calvin Coolidge but paid no further mind. Elsie wholeheartedly threw her support behind Joe Beemish, as did the powerful Ada Nesterud.

17. The End of Prohibition

The repeal of Prohibition enforced by the Twenty-first Amendment brought an important date to Gem City, one that would forever be remembered by all Gem Citians, young and old: 1933.

A massive celebration was planned at Gem City's largest picnic area, Felix Nelson Memorial Park. Some folks didn't understand the logical reasoning behind the idea for a celebration, since almost no one adhered to Prohibition anyway.

There were many speeches that day. Among which, were former Mayor Elsie Nelson's poignant words, "I only wish my dear husband Felix were here to see this."

Mayor Beemish took the podium to announce the beginning of the celebration and an end to the ham-fisted demagoguery of Minnesota Congressman, Andrew J. Volstead, and his followers. The crowd responded with hisses and boos at the mention of his name.

There were cheers when Beemish dramatically read the picnic menu. "There's plenty of beer and Canadian whiskey." Above the din of eardrum-shattering hoots, hollers and whistling, hardly anyone heard him say that there were also hotdogs, potato salad, apple pie and lemonade for the kids. "Enough for everyone," he beamed.

The party finally wound down in the young hours of the next day. The Fire Department was dispatched to hose down the near acre of used hotdogs, potato salad on the grass, and pools of urine on the flagstone floor of the pavilion.

18. Elsie, Stella and Ed

Elsie Nelson sat in her rocking chair listening to the radio. Lately, she hadn't been feeling well. She had "good" days and "bad" days, and on this Saturday in early Spring, she was having one of her "good" days.

It's a small miracle that I'm still alive, she thought. *But Spring has arrived, the snow is receding, and buds are popping out on the trees.*

The afternoon sun was bright, and Elsie had to avert her eyes from time to time. She found the slow rhythm of her rocking chair comforting when she was alone—just sitting there in her quilted, pink and blue housecoat and worn out slippers.

"Momma, Momma guess what?" Eighteen-year-old Stella came running into the house, breathlessly. "Oh, here's your Chesterfields and your bottle of beer. Grain Belt okay?"

"Thank you, dear. Can you open it for me?"

"Guess what? Ed Benson asked me to marry him!"

Elsie turned off the radio. "Just a little bit of Kaltenborn can go a long way. Now what didja say?"

"Ed, you know, Ed Benson, asked me to marry him?"

"What happened to that little Italian boy you were runnin' with?"

"That was high school, Momma."

"Do I know this Benson guy?"

"You can meet him this evening. I invited him over for supper. He's waiting in the car. We're gonna take in a matinee. Some John Wayne movie, I guess."

"Well, dear, it's either gonna be a war picture, or a western. I can't stand all that shooting and killing! Anyway, where's your engagement ring?"

"Oh, he can't afford one right now, but he's been looking for a job ever since he got out of the Navy."

"The damn war's been over for three years! What's he been doin'?"

"Just odd jobs, but it don't matter. He wants to be an engineer."

"That's good. The railroad needs good men. But he'll probably hafta start at the bottom."

"Yeah, Momma, like porter, or somethin'"

"Stella, that's what they got colored boys for."

"Okay, then, brakeman, or signalman, or whatever you call 'em."

"And where do ya think you're gonna live, Mrs. Stella Benson?"

"Why, right here with you, Momma. That is till Ed gets that job. Then, I suppose we'll settle in Gem City. Ed likes Gem City."

"You can have the whole damn house when I'm dead, which won't be too long now."

"You shouldn't talk that way, Momma."

"Well, you better hurry up and get married, 'cause I'm sinkin' fast. I can feel it."

"We're gettin' married in June, that's only two months away. I gotta go, or we'll be late for the movie. Now get dressed and I'll be back to cook supper.

"You know, Momma, you should really try to get some exercise. Just sitting there drinking beer and smokin' cigarettes ain't good for you."

"I get enough exercise sittin' in this rocker and getting up to go to the toilet."

Ed was just getting out of the car when Stella bounded out of the house.

Elsie's two other daughters, Mary, who lived in Milwaukee, and Margaret in Seattle, both started writing to their mother, after Felix's demise.

Would they be able to come for Stella's wedding? Or my funeral? Whatever comes first, I suppose.

Mary and Margaret left their husbands and children behind and took trains to Gem City, in time for Elsie's funeral. They both stayed long enough to be bridesmaids at Stella's wedding.

Elsie was buried next to Felix, along with her terrible secret. She'd thought about telling Stella what had happened to her father but decided against it with no regrets. One of the few regrets Elsie had, was never getting to meet her four grandchildren. A fifth grandchild, a girl, was born the following Spring. Ed and Stella Benson named her Barbara.

19. Warren Pease

T
he Pease family moved to Gem City in the late 1940s. Mike and Rose Pease both worked second shift at Gem City Cartridge, the munitions plant on the southeast end of town. They had a married daughter living in Jersey City, New Jersey, and two sons. Mike, Jr. was a high school senior and ten-year-old Warren was in grade school.

Mike and Rose unwittingly named their youngest son, Warren, after Rose's favorite brother. They didn't realize that everyone else had heard of the Tolstoy novel—even if they had never read it.

Warren always seemed to know when supposedly mature adults were laughing at his name behind his back. So, he chose and started using his middle name, Eugene Pease didn't sound much better. It made the school kids laugh in his face. He shortened Eugene to Gene. That wasn't much of an improvement, either.

Because of Gene's uncanny gift for mimicry, he was able to easily make friends by entertaining them. He could imitate every teacher in the whole school, including the principal. He could do some actors as well: Gary Cooper, Clark Gable and Cary Grant. His favorite and best was Humphrey Bogart. Unfortunately, when Gene reached high school, he was spending more time honing his impressions than doing his schoolwork.

Something terrible happened on September 30, 1955. The teen world was shaken by the news of actor James Dean's tragic death. Every teenager, whether they had a rebellious thought in their heads or not, reacted in horror, shock and grief. Gene Pease reached a little deeper, emotionally and decided to quit school about a month later. He cut a picture of Dean's car crash out of the newspaper and carried it in his wallet. The picture showed Dean's crumpled, aluminum Porsche, the Little Bastard, with a pair of legs, presumably Dean's, sticking out from under the wreckage.

Gene practiced screaming, "You're tearing me apart!" Then, having perfected the line, he tried it out on his parents. They thought he was having a nervous breakdown and feared for his mental health.

He repeatedly saw "Rebel Without a Cause" at the Ruby Theater. Finally, he started wearing a red cloth jacket, white t-shirt and blue jeans, just like Dean wore in the Rebel movie. He even started combing his hair like Dean. Other than that, Gene didn't look anything like James Dean.

He vowed to himself, that every year, on the anniversary of Dean's death, he'd make the pilgrimage to Indiana and camp-out next to James Byron Dean's grave. Gene never did this because something called maturity took hold of him. He left home and hitchhiked to Minneapolis. Rose and Mike knew where Gene had gone but didn't go after him. They soon had more tragic events to cope with.

Their daughter Nancy and her husband were standing on a subway platform, waiting for a train, when Nancy leaned over to see the sign on an oncoming train and fell off the platform. She was run over and killed by the wrong train. It was going to Trenton.

About a week later, they learned that their oldest son had died when he fell from a ladder, while painting the trim on his house. By anyone's standards, Mike Jr. was grossly overweight. He weighed around three-hundred pounds and was only five-feet-four, so he didn't carry it very well. He had fallen on his stomach and died.

Soon after his arrival in Minneapolis, Gene was befriended, given food and shelter by an evangelist preacher named, Clyde Perkins. Perkins was a light-skinned, biracial man or, as people said in those days, a mulatto. He was also a closeted homosexual. Gene wasn't really a homosexual, but he had a predilection, together with a sexual ambivalence, to lean toward Clyde's way of life. Besides, he felt that he had to somehow repay his benefactor.

Reverend Perkins was a tall, rail-thin man with black, wavy hair and a thin, black mustache. He kind of looked like Sal Mineo—a perfect match for Gene's, James Dean persona.

Perkins owned a small, white, nondenominational chapel and held services on Friday nights and Sunday mornings. Non-members would sometimes ask the Reverend if he had been ordained. He'd get a peevish expression on his face, then bellow that he was ordained by God, Himself. He was a very attractive man, so the female congregants of his church would congregate around him; women always asked him over for supper and so forth. Occasionally, he would take them up on it. But he reserved his most lavish attention for Gene Pease.

Perkins was a gifted musician, so he taught Gene how to play the old Baptist hymns on the piano. Gene began playing for all the church services.

Perkins bought Gene clothes and one day surprised Gene by buying him a car of his own. As time went on, the two men acted more like colleagues, than anything else. They kept their other relationship secret.

Tragedy wasn't yet finished with the Pease family. With all their children gone, Mike and Rose would either argue all the time, or they wouldn't speak to each other for days at a time. One morning when they weren't speaking to each other, Rose had a doctor's appointment in St. Stephen. Since Rose didn't drive, Mike had to drive her. He took their old Plymouth up Main Street to the state highway and turned east. Mike took the right turn a little wide and didn't see the eighteen-wheeler because of a blinding sunrise that day. The last thing Mike and Rose heard was the throaty blast of the truck's airhorn, and the last thing they saw was the word, "Freightliner" in chrome, block letters.

Meanwhile, Gene couldn't help having several covert affairs with women. Sometimes, he stayed out and missed the Friday night service. Word got around to the Reverend that Gene had been seen in the company of women on Hennepin Avenue. Perkins had no other recourse, but to tell Gene that he had to leave. Gene bought a train ticket back to Gem City.

20. Gene, Natalie and Wendy

I t wasn't until Gene happened to bump into an old friend from high school, that he found out he was his family's sole heir. He never could stand the old Pease house, so he sold it.

With the money from the sale, together with the money he had saved, he purchased the vacant Sinclair's Standard Oil gas station. He had it remodeled, making it larger, adding a small convenience store where the mechanics' bays used to be. He named the store, Qik Stop. He also added three more gas pumps, eventually replacing all of them with newer, more modern-looking ones. He had the sign repainted, "Gene's Standard Oil."

With his first gasoline delivery, in time for his grand opening, Standard Oil provided him with brand new advertising signs. As expected, his first customers were his old school buddies. They still saw him as a charismatic figure—the sort of rebel they'd always longed to be.

Gene Pease leaned against one of his new gas pumps at his station. It was sunrise and already he could hear the roar of heavy earth-moving equipment and men shouting orders at each other.

Knowing that his gas station wasn't part of the city's revitalization project, he thought that new businesses and homes would be just the thing to help Gem City get back on its feet. Besides, new activity would be good for his business. Certainly, all the heavy trucks were stopping in for diesel fuel and soon, more people would be moving to Gem City and buying more gas to get someplace else. Life was good and getting better. It was 1962 and Gene felt on top of the world since Natalie and Wendy came along.

Gene first met Natalie Rollwitz and her nine-year old daughter, Wendy, the summer of 1959, when they stopped for gas and for directions to St. Stephen. He learned that Natalie was a divorcee from Minneapolis and was planning to look for a job in St. Stephen.

Gene cordially invited them inside the Qik Stop to look around. He had decorated the walls with James Dean posters and Porsche insignias. This struck Natalie as a little odd, but interesting. One entire wall was blank except for three eight-by-ten black and white photos sharing one black frame. Hand printed underneath the pictures was a date: February 3, 1959.

"Do you know who these guys are?" Gene asked.

"Sure," Natalie answered, "it's Ritchie Valens, J.P. 'The Big Bopper' Richardson and Buddy Holly."

"Even I know who they are." Wendy chimed in.

Natalie asked Gene, "Is that the day they died?"

"Killed would be more like it. First, Elvis gets drafted, then this. I think it'll finish Rock 'n' Roll."

Natalie was anxious to leave and asked Gene if he knew of any jobs available in St. Stephen.

"No, but there might be a job opening in Gem City."

"Where in Gem City?"

"Right here at the Qik Stop. I pump gas all day and you run the cash register and the store. How does that sound?"

"I don't know. What do you think, Wendy?"

"I guess it sounds okay, but where are we gonna live?"

"I've got a spare room that I'm using for storage, but I can move that junk out."

"Oh, but Gene, I just don't want a lot of people to know that Wendy and I are here. I've got an ex. You know what I mean?"

"Gotcha."

Natalie's fears were never realized. She didn't see or hear from her ex again.

That fall, Wendy started the fifth grade at Penn Elementary. One day she came home crying her eyes out. It seemed that some of the kids in school had figured out that her parents weren't married because they had different last names. A few weeks later, Gene and Natalie were married in a civil ceremony at the St. Stephen County Courthouse.

Gene decided that Pease wasn't a proper last name for Wendy or Natalie, nor for himself for that matter. So, he, Natalie and Wendy had their names changed. Their new family name, from then on, was Dean, in honor of Gene's fixation with James Dean.

Gene was happy with the simple rhyme of his name. Natalie liked it because, coupled with her first name, it sounded like wind chimes. The kids at school started calling Wendy, "Dee Dee."

Everything was going pretty well for the Deans until one rainy spring day Natalie looked out the window of the store and called for Gene.

"Gene, Gene, look at what's going on over there!"

"What? I can't believe it! They're tearing down Colonel Parks's house!"

They were watching a wrecking ball hit the side of the old house, when a car pulled up outside. A young man and an older man got out and came into the store. "Well, whaddya think?" the older man asked. "Do ya know what's goin' in over there?"

"No, what?"

"A ten-pump Texaco station with a three-bay garage. We're gonna sell automotive supplies, too. Oh, by the way, my name's Lyle Houlegaard and this is my boy, Bob. Looks like we're gonna be competitors."

Lyle and Bob were still grinning when Gene pulled a switchblade from his pocket and flicked out a four-inch blade. Gene always believed that there was a time and place for everything, time for peace and a time for violence. He didn't normally believe in violence, but in this situation, he reasoned, violence would be Lyle Houlegaard's key to understanding.

"Now would be a good time for the two of you to get the hell out of here," Gene growled.

Lyle and Bob pushed each other out of the way as they ran to their car and sped away, tires screeching.

Gene had to do some jail time for that, but he thought it was worth it.

During construction of the sprawling Texaco station, one of the bulldozers backed into the World War Two monument at War Memorial Point, causing it to fall over and break; the tallest of the four monuments, it was a rectangular monolith made of polished black marble inscribed with names of servicemen from Gem City killed in the war.

A district court judge ordered Houlegaard and the construction company to replace the monument with an exact duplicate. In order to afford the expense, Houlegaard had to raise gasoline prices higher than Gene's. He also took out a second mortgage on his house. The real damage had already been done and Houlegaard, suddenly unpopular for damaging the monument, lost most of his business right from the start.

There was a re-dedication ceremony at the War Memorial presided over by the Mayor, a short, red-faced man with a lisp. In his speech, the Mayor read off each name appearing on the World War Two marker. There were forty-two names of sons, husbands, fathers, brothers and boyfriends. That was quite a few, out of a pre-war population of eleven thousand. The Korean War had also been memorialized with a square block of granite. There were no names on that one.

The ceremony wasn't like the gatherings Gem City used to have. This time, only a few people turned out. They yawned and politely applauded once in a while. The Houlegaards were conspicuously absent from the ceremony that day.

Ada Nesterud had noted that after the original World War Two monument was installed that perhaps there should be just one large monument for all the wars, past, as well as future. She was certain there would be more.

21. Friday, November 22, 1963

High school freshman Wendy Dean came home early from school the day President Kennedy was assassinated. Gene and Natalie closed the gas station early.

"They murdered the president in broad daylight," said Gene, tears streaming down his cheeks, "in front of hundreds of people. What the hell's this country coming to?"

Our Lady of the River Catholic Church was planning to hold a special mass, that evening, inviting people of all faiths to attend. Catholics and Lutherans alike, were surprised at Monsignor Lisowski's gesture, considering the decades-old animosity which existed since quarreling about their church's names.

Our Lady of the River was packed to the rafters that night. The Methodist minister from St. Mark's and the young pastor from St. Stephen Lutheran were there. The young pastor stood in front of the sanctuary with the other two sad old men whose faces were taut and ashen. They tried not to make eye contact with each other, nervously staring at the ceiling instead, shifting from one foot to the other, waiting for the service to begin.

The clergymen delivered eulogies to the fallen leader. The sounds of muffled sobs could be heard, echoing around the cavernous sanctuary. Anger, fear and sadness gripped the night.

Most of the town turned out at the church after most businesses closed early. The Deans, especially Gene, noticed that the Texaco station remained open. It was yet another reason for Gene to hate Lyle Houlegaard.

Part III

22. Bob Peterson Returns to Gem City

Working for the Pinkerton Agency did not keep Gem City's erstwhile Chief of Police busy enough to distract him from thinking about the unsolved Benson murder case. Bob Peterson spent endless sleepless nights at the kitchen table, reviewing details of the cold case, scribbling notes, chain-smoking and drinking coffee. Sleep, he figured, only delayed his thought processes. *There has to be something we missed*, he mumbled over and over to himself.

His job as a Minneapolis Operations Manager meant that he had to ensure all Pinkerton accounts were fully staffed. He was able to staff many of the accounts with college students seeking temporary employment in the spring. As he did every morning, Bob scanned the *Tribune*. That particular morning, in the section covering regional events, a story about Gem City caught his attention.

Two weeks earlier, on May 3rd, three force five tornadoes had danced across St. Stephen County and struck Gem City hardest. *The poor bastards, they're still digging out and finding bodies.*

U.S. Senator Hubert Horatio Humphrey stated that Gem City might qualify for federal disaster relief. Bob shook the paper and blinked as he read to the bottom of the column. "Gem City," the article concluded, "is also known for the grisly murder of a teenaged girl, whose case remains unsolved nearly four years later."

Business had leveled off, so Bob arranged to take a two-week vacation. He told his wife Ruthie that he was going up to Gem City for two or three days, to look around at the mess the tornadoes left. But he had another reason: Barbara Benson. Her unsolved murder was the event that convinced him to retire and leave Gem City.

Driving north on the state highway, he remembered how long and boring the trip was—nothing but flatland, continuous rows of corn, wheat and potato fields until he reached the outskirts of Gem City. There was something he didn't understand about the strange, little town. Every street except Main came to a dead end. This turned out pretty well if you were a cop involved in a car chase. All the police had to do was setup roadblocks on the ends of Main Street.

Peterson turned onto Main Street and noticed that three beer joints had survived the tornadoes. One sign read, "Live Entertainment Weekends." They had a four-piece Polka band and a jukebox that played sad country songs on 45s, mostly Hank Williams. Another joint had a sign that read, "No Dancing, No Shirt, No Shoes; No Service, No Credit."

Bob turned right onto Fifth Avenue, which served as an extension of the business district. He stopped, and from the avenue, he could see the redeveloped site of the old Parks Baseball Field. He reminisced quickly about all the exciting games played there.

Company teams, The Bullets and The Steelers, played on that field. Then there was the fantastic city team, The Diamonds; and the high school team, The Gems, conference champs, four years in a row. Bob had heard that during World War Two some of the women, housewives and factory workers got together and formed their own team, The Garnettes, a team every bit as good as the men's teams. After the war, the women's team disbanded.

Then, someone had the brilliant idea that the land occupying the ballfield was not being utilized for its "highest and best use."

The developers forgot, or perhaps they didn't really forget, that the old ballpark was constructed on soft landfill, and they went ahead and built new townhomes. The townhomes now stood vacant, leaning like drunken dominoes. The only thing that kept some of them from falling completely over was that they leaned against each other for support.

Bob made a U-turn and headed back toward Main but stopped near the front of the library to study the graffiti on one of the cracked stucco walls. Someone had spray-painted a six-pointed star with a circle around it, along with some illegible wording. He squinted at one word. It looked to be "Satan" or "Satanic." *Stupid kids! They meant to draw a pentagram, but the morons drew a Star of David. What a buncha ignorant jerkoffs.* There was an Open sign on the library door, but Bob saw no one going in or coming out.

He focused his attention on the rectangular, one-story building across the street. Vacant. Duct tape across the cracks of the large, plate-glass storefront. It had formerly been the Gem City Bakery for almost as many years as Bob had lived and worked in Gem City.

Old, crusty men, retired farmers, merchants, and laborers gathered there every morning for a breakfast of doughnuts, strong black coffee, cigarettes and pipe tobacco. They'd come in and push two long tables together and settle in for discussions regarding the fate of Gem City along with the rest of Western Civilization.

They lounged there, some with ill-fitting dentures, some without any teeth, smoking, drinking coffee and eating doughnuts. Whenever one of them told a joke, they all broke into uncontrolled laughter, including the joke-teller, wheezy, emphysematous, coughing fits. This would invariably cause some of them to cough up gelatinous hunks of brackish phlegm the size of Kennedy half-dollars, which they'd daintily wipe from their tongues with paper napkins.

Wearing their dingy ball caps covering dirty, matted, uncombed hair, or balding heads, they talked about serious things like the Vietnam War. Most of them agreed, having seen war and hating war, that the current one should end soon, but were careful not to join ranks with the hippies, protesters and draft-dodgers. Although, they assured each other that none of them had voted for Nixon, they believed Nixon when he said he had a "secret plan" to end the war. He would later say that it was merely "campaign rhetoric," the kind of hyperbole that gets men elected to the highest public office in the land.

You knew when you entered the bakery that the old boys had been in there because the acrid, gray-blue tobacco smoke hung down from the ceiling to about three-feet off the floor. The nicotine mass only moved slightly when someone walked by. Small wonder that everything from the bakery smelled and tasted as if were smoke cured.

Sitting in his car across the street in his reverie, Peterson recalled that the police would sometimes have to go into the bakery and roust the old guys out of there, telling them that they were expected home for lunch. Of course, the widowers could stay as long as they wanted.

The bakery appeared untouched by the tornadoes. It had simply gone out of business and the old guys were either displaced or had died. Bob cleared those thoughts and pulled away from the curb. His next stop would be Gem City's version of Forest Lawn,

Gethsemane Cemetery.

As he wheeled up Main Street, Peterson observed low, swift-moving clouds drifting across the south. It probably means rain. He wanted to get some things done before that happened.

There wasn't much movement in town that day, except for an old man bending over to examine a small piece of debris. He kicked it aside, straightened up and stared blankly as Bob drove by.

The former police chief slowed down to look up at a large hawk chasing a sparrow. Even though he was rooting for the sparrow, with its agile, evasive maneuvering, he knew that the odds were in the hawk's favor. He had to make an evasive maneuver himself, to avoid an empty cigarette machine lying on its side at the curb.

Groups of men from the phone company and the power company, all wearing hard hats, stood around their trucks talking and waving their arms, oblivious of Bob's blue Chevy picking up speed, headed north toward the cemetery.

City Hall, a limestone building, appeared on the right. Some of the windows were broken. The lights were off and it looked to be vacant. A stub of what used to be a flagpole stood alongside. Bob stopped his car to look at the former home to the police department until the county took over. The fire department still operated out of the lower level. Chiseled into the limestone archway above the main entrance were the words, "GEM CITY CITY HALL." Bob laughed to himself, as many people did, at the apparent redundancy of the word, "City."

A prearranged visit with Johnny Briggs, the caretaker at the cemetery, was one of Bob's real reasons for coming back to Gem City. He pulled up to the open wrought iron gate. A National Guard MP approached him and growled, "Can I help you, sir?" His kind offer of assistance belied a surly attitude; that and the fact that he held an M-16 at port arms.

"I'm here to see Mr. Briggs," Bob explained, gesturing toward the cemetery office.

"He's inside," said the MP, seemingly disappointed at not having an opportunity to shoot somebody.

Briggs came out of the office and shouted, "Bob, you made it!"

"Good to see ya, Johnny. How've ya been?"

"Been better, been worse."

"What the hell's the National Guard still doing here?"

"Right now, they're taking down that old elm tree that was hit by the tornado. See that guy standing there in the suit? He's a city councilman."

"What's he doing, supervising?"

"He's making sure that they cut the branches into one-foot lengths."

"What for?"

"He's gonna load it in his pickup and haul it down to City Hall and sell it for firewood."

"Sorry I asked."

"That backhoe over there is gonna start digging graves for the tornado victims—about fifty, maybe more."

"That many, huh?"

"Yeah, hopefully some of 'em will be cremated."

"Shit, Johnny, this is a lot worse than the tornado in '65."

"That was just a baby compared to three F-5s! Let's go inside the office."

Johnny Briggs was a small, wiry man in his mid-seventies, one of only a few Black men in Gem City. Johnny loved to tell the story of how, following World War Two, he migrated to Gem City from St. Paul after losing his job when thousands of servicemen returned from the war. He took the train up to Gem City, where he heard they were hiring at the foundry and the munitions plant.

The personnel manager at the foundry bluntly told him that he was too old. He didn't even get in to see anybody at the munitions plant. Then, someone told him about Ada Nesterud, the city councilwoman, a New Dealer and Gem City's answer to Eleanor Roosevelt.

Johnny told Mrs. Nesterud about his difficulty finding a job and that he wanted to get spiffed-up with a haircut for job interviews, but the barber refused to do it.

"'Johnny,' she smiled, 'go back, get that haircut and go over to the cemetery office. The old guy there needs an assistant.' As I was goin' out the door, she was on the phone, yellin' at the barber."

Bob pretended not to remember that it was he-himself who told Johnny to see Mrs. Nesterud in the first place.

"She got me this job. Ada Nesterud was the best thing that ever happened to me and this town. What a fine lady. The best.

"You know, Bob," Johnny waxed, philosophically, "God made us all equal when we're born and equal when we die. It's the shit that happens in between, that's all fucked up. They're all here," he waved his arm toward the gravestones, "the philanderers, the crooks, the wife-beaters, the closet alcoholics. You bury the whole damn closet, along with the skeletons."

"There's some good people too," Bob interjected.

"Oh, yeah, like Mrs. Nesterud."

"Johnny, I gotta get down to business. Since I haven't been here in a while, I forgot where the Bensons' are buried."

"The Bensons. Yeah, we had newspaper reporters, TV crime reporters and tourists wanting to see where they were buried, right after it happened, the murders. Let's see, they're over there by that pine tree. Three flat markers next to the big monument that says, 'Nelson.' In case you didn't know, Stella Benson's maiden name was Nelson. Her daddy was mayor of Gem City. I'd go over there and show you, but this goddam weather is playin' havoc with my knees."

"That's okay Johnny, I'll find 'em. Hey, thanks a lot."

Bob started walking over to the pine tree, trying to ignore the MP who was still standing at the gate, watching Bob's every move. Bob came up to one of the largest monuments, a granite hunk with the simple inscription, "Colonel Jack Parks, 1870-1929. U.S. Army, Spanish-American War." There was a horseshoe bolted to the top of the marker.

Next to the Parks' grave stood a marble monument marking Ada Nesterud' final resting place. Instead of her birth and death dates, the inscription noted her years on the city council, "1920-1956." This didn't strike Bob, or anyone else as odd because practically everyone who knew her knew that she would have things exactly the way she wanted, even in death.

Okay, there's Nelson, and here's the Bensons, all three of them dead the same year, 1966, a few days after their daughter, Barbara. There's nothing here, but it might help knowing that Stella Benson was homegrown.

He turned to walk away and saw in the distance a marker with the family name of "Pease." It reminded him that he had to talk with Gene Dean, owner of "Gene's Standard and Qik Stop." His daughter, Wendy, had gone to school with Barb Benson. Bob especially wanted to talk to her.

Bob headed south on Main Street for Gene's. He pulled up at one of the gas pumps. Gene Dean came out of the store and recognized Peterson right away. Gene yelled, laughing, his arms raised, "I'm innocent! I didn't do it!"

"Yes you did, but it ain't a crime to be a horse's ass."

"What brings you back, Bob? Want a fill-up?"

"Sure. Oh, I just came up to snoop around. Heard about the tornadoes. Terrible!"

Looking over at the boarded-up Texaco station, Bob asked, "Did the Texaco go out of business?"

"The tornadoes put 'em out of business, what little business they had. We're all havin' a hard time, Bob."

"How's your wife? Natalie, isn't it?"

"She's fine."

"How 'bout Wendy? She still around?"

"Yeah. She's a junior at St. Cloud, out on spring break. She helps me here and then goes over to City Hall. Since she's a math major, the city gave her the job of Finance Director."

"I was thinking about Wendy being in the same class with Barb Benson. Is it okay if I talk to her?"

"Don't ask me, ask her. She's over at City Hall, right now."

"Hey, do you remember that fracas you had with Houlegaard? You pulled a knife on him and I had to arrest you. What'd you do, go nuts or something?"

"No, why?"

"Never mind. God, I remember the first time I met you, Gene. It was right after you breezed back into town. I pulled you over for speeding but for some reason, decided not to tag you. Then I noticed that you weren't wearing your seatbelt, so I told you that old bromide about my never having to unbuckle a dead man. Remember what you said to me?"

"Nope, I don't"

"You said, 'Why the hell would a dead guy be wearin' a seatbelt?' Man, I felt like climbing in that car after you and raising some knots on your head. Are you over that attitude problem?"

Gene laughed, "What attitude problem?"

They both laughed until Gene got serious and lamented, "This town's nothing now. Did you see the population sign? Unbelievable. It's down to 1,700 people! Nobody cares anymore. Turning into a ghost town. Businesses that weren't flattened by the tornados, either went out of business or moved somewhere else."

"A lot of small towns are getting that way."

"By the way, Bob, I'm the mayor now. Narrowly made it the first time. It was something. Some guy decided to run for mayor and his wife ran for city council. The thing was, they'd just moved here. How could they possibly know all the intricacies of Gem City?"

Bob smiled and shook his head, "Damned if I know, Gene. You're the mayor?"

"Yeah, I was re-elected the last time by a landslide. Ran unopposed. People just aren't interested in what's goin' on, anymore. The city council's been cut back to three members, including the mayor. After this term, Natalie's gonna run for mayor. After that, I suppose it'll be Wendy's turn. I'm tellin' you Bob, people are moving away, abandoning their homes even. Nobody ever stops here anymore. Gas prices are sky-high, and I just can't afford to stay in business."

"Don't you collect a salary for being mayor?"

"Yeah, but not for long. The town's almost broke. I suppose you heard they had to shut down all the schools."

"What happened?"

Gene went on to explain that the school district had tried to raise money for a new high school gymnasium. Voters overwhelmingly defeated the school bond referendum, and since there was no other way to raise money, the school began to cut extracurricular activities.

"The football was first to be cut, which was no great tragedy. Then basketball, still nothing too tragic. Then, the unimaginable happened, the city's shut down our beloved baseball program. The school's baseball team quickly became defunct. Parents and kids both decided that going to school in St. Stephen, where they at least still played baseball, was the better option. Enrollment declined so fast that the Gem City school board decided to close all the schools,

K-through-12. The board members voted themselves out of a job. St. Stephen High School welcomed the idea and even built another glass case for all the Gem City Gems baseball trophies."

Bob and Dean shook hands and parted. Bob was on his way to see Wendy. Gene had phoned her and said that Bob would be stopping over, probably to talk about Barb Benson.

Peterson drove a short distance to City Hall and parked in the asphalt lot behind the building, completely vacant except for a Ford Fairlane, which he concluded belonged to Wendy Dean. He noticed that she had parked in the space he used when he was Chief-of-Police.

All the lights were off inside. Bob headed for the stairway to offices on the second floor. Wendy waited for him at the top of the stairs. "Hi, Mr. Peterson. The power's still off in here. C'mon up."

Wendy had changed into a fully-grown woman, which surprised Peterson. Her short, dish-water blond hair, it seemed to Bob, only added to her plain looks, though by no means was she unattractive. Wendy wore a bright-green pullover sweater and faded, bellbottom, blue jeans. "Well, hello to you," said Bob with a big smile.

"You want to ask me some things about Barb Benson? Let's talk then, while we still have some natural light up here. Can I bum a cigarette from you? I'd offer you some coffee, except that I can't make any."

Bob lit a cigarette and began the thirteen-step climb. "What're you doing over here, Wendy? Helping the mayor?"

"Yeah, I'm trying to get a finance report done for Dad. I've gotta go back to school tomorrow."

"Your dad said that you were home for spring break?"

"He doesn't know what he's talking about. I've been home all summer working here and at the store. Let's go to my office and I'll tell you everything I remember about the Benson girl, which isn't much."

"Any little bit helps, Wendy."

"By the way, Mr. Peterson …"

"… Call me Bob."

"Okay, Bob. I want you to know that my dad didn't appreciate being one of your suspects. I mean, just because he was sort of rowdy in his youth, doesn't mean, you know, doesn't equate to murder. Besides, he had, my family had an alibi. We were home either watching TV or sleeping."

"I know and your dad was the first suspect we cleared."

"Fine."

"Can we get down to business, now, Wendy? I've heard for a long time that Barb was different from other girls in school."

"That she was. I had different boyfriends all through school, but I don't recall ever seeing Barb in the company of a boy."

"Did you consider yourself one of her friends?"

"Acquaintance would be more like it. I mean, we weren't close. We'd talk in the halls and sometimes have lunch together. Stuff like that, but not close. It was awful what happened to her, though. Who'd want to kill her? She didn't hurt anybody."

"Would you describe her as a loner?"

"She was friendly enough, but yes, I'd say she generally kept to herself."

"When was the last time you saw her alive?"

"Let's see. She was killed on a Saturday night. Right? I saw her walking from school on that Friday afternoon."

"Was she alone?"

"Funny you ask. No, she was with another girl. I remember, it was Vicky Skalicki."

"Who the hell is Vicki Skalicky? I don't remember interviewing her at the school that day."

"You didn't. Vicky moved out of town and dropped out of school soon after Barb was killed. I don't know where she moved to. What I don't understand, Bob, is that Vicki was a popular girl. Why would she associate with an unpopular girl like Barb Benson?"

"Don't know. Maybe she felt sorry for her."

"Another thing I don't get—Vicki had been going steady with John Anderson."

"Now, who's John Anderson?"

"John graduated a year ahead of us. Up until that time, he and Vicki were inseparable. I mean, joined at the hip. They went to every school dance. You didn't see one without the other. I was good friends with both of them."

"So, what happened to him?"

"He joined the Air Force. They sent him to Viet Nam and that's when she broke up with him. When she told me, I was shocked! She said it would be too long to wait for him. I don't know if any of this helps you."

"It does. Thanks a lot, Wendy. That's all I have for now. Let's keep in touch, in case you think of anything else."

"Wait a sec, Bob. Wouldn't the Skalicky girl be a suspect? One of the last people seen with her?"

"Killed, like in a fit of jealous rage or something? I don't think so."

"Why not? Don't you think that girls are capable of committing murder?"

"Girls killing girls," Bob said dismissively. He lit another cigarette. "Girls killing girls, Wendy?"

Wendy shook her head. "Yeah, well, look, I've got a ton of work to do." She pulled a green ledger from a stack in front of her. "We're supposed to get that federal aid package, but we're not really counting on getting it anytime soon. So I'm trying to apply it to next year's budget, if there is a next year. Could you give me a couple more cigarettes before you leave?"

Bob gave her the pack. He had more in the glove compartment. Their conversation was over. He walked over to a phone sitting on a vacant desk. "You mind if I make a call?"

"No. Oh, wait a minute, Bob! I've got to call that National Guard guy, Major what's his face, and tell him you're leaving. They've been watching you, ever since you got here."

"Yeah, they weren't trying to hide it."

Wendy dialed the phone on her desk and murmured something about a navy-blue, late model Chevy.

Peterson called his former colleague and nemesis, Captain Dennis Hanson, at his office in St. Stephen. Bob had talked to him a week earlier and said that he'd call him again when he reached Gem City, hinting that there might be some new evidence in the Benson murder case. Hanson of course was anxious to schedule a meeting. There was no new evidence, but Bob had a gut feeling about the old evidence. After the brief phone conversation, they agreed to meet at Ski's Bar and Grill in St. Stephen, at 5:30 p.m. after Hanson got off work.

"Wendy, I gotta go. It's been nice seeing you again, and what you told about Barb not walking home alone was very helpful."

"Thanks," Wendy said as she looked up from her ledgers, managing a faint smile. "Yeah, call me at my dorm, if you can think of any more questions."

23. Peterson Reunites with Captain Hanson

B ob waited for Hanson at Ski's Bar in St. Stephen for an hour and-a-half during which time he gulped four whiskey sours and devoured a cheeseburger. When Hanson finally took a seat in Peterson's booth, he said, "Sorry I'm late, Chief. Got tied up; we're kinda busy. It's good to see you. You haven't changed a hair; haven't grown any new ones either."

"You were always real funny, Dennis."

"You said you've got something for me about Benson?"

"Well, I was thinking that if we had to, we could get those bodies exhumed and give them proper autopsies instead of the hack job Shephard did. That crazy shit."

"Exhume the bodies? You're pulling my leg, right? We can't dig up the whole family."

"Maybe it won't be necessary, but if push comes to shove, Dennis, we can get a court order."

"You got new evidence?"

"I want to rummage through your evidence room. There might be something we overlooked."

"I'm not gonna reopen a cold case based on a hunch."

"Look, if we don't find anything, the case stays cold. Fair enough? Just let me look."

"Okay, okay. Come by my office first thing in the morning and we'll look at the evidence together. Say, how much did you have to drink? Can I drive you to a motel?"

"I'm staying at the hotel across the street."

"Oh. Good. Don't want you driving. See you tomorrow then."

"Hey Dennis, whatever happened to the Gem City Hotel?"

"Don't you remember? Holiday Inn bought it. They just finished remodeling when the tornado hit it. Total loss."

"Aw, geez."

It was raining the next morning, not hard and steady, but off and on. Peterson met Hanson and they took the elevator to the basement of the courthouse. It was a cold, damp place. Down the hall from the morgue and the jail, the two men entered the evidence room.

"I had one of the deputies dig out the boxes with the Benson stuff. Over there are the file cabinets with the case paperwork. Since there's no statute of limitation for murder cases, these items will remain here till somebody solves the case."

"Somebody might. Now, let's take a look at what we got here."

Hanson pulled the lid off one of the boxes. "We kept the clothes they were wearing when they died. That's mostly what's in here. We've also got the .22, .38 and .357 slugs that Shephard dug from their bodies."

"I wanna see Ed Benson's things first."

Hanson removed Ed Benson's suit from a clear plastic evidence bag and laid it on a long metal table. Benson's suit, which he had worn to his daughter's funeral. Almost every inch of it was stiff with dried blood the color of dark rust.

Hanson handed Bob Stella's dress, which was also matted with dried blood. Some of the creases were stuck together. The former Chief barely glanced at it. "Dennis, do you remember the Alfred Hitchcock TV show, the one about a woman bashing her husband's brains out with a frozen leg of lamb, then inviting the cops to stay for dinner?"

"Yeah, and they ate the leg of lamb, right? So how's that analogous to this case? Did somebody eat the murder weapon?"

"No, college boy. I'm just saying that the murder weapon is probably right here under out very noses, right in this room."

"I think you need some fresh air, Bob." Hanson led the way outside. They walked around the block smoking cigarettes. The rain had stopped; the sun came out. Back at the courthouse on a warm September morning, the veteran detectives stopped on the way to the basement for coffee from a vending machine.

A young female receptionist rushed over. "Oh, Mr. Peterson, while you were out you got a message from somebody named Wendy Dean."

"What was the message?"

"She wants you to call her back."

"I'd better call her, Dennis. It'll only be a minute."

Wendy answered the phone in a flat monotone. "Gem City City Hall."

"Bob Peterson, Wendy."

"Bob, Viki Skalicky was the name of the girl with Barb Benson after school the day Barb was killed."

"We interviewed dozens of kids at the high school. I don't recall any Vicki Skalicky."

Hanson mimed to Bob that he was going to finish his coffee outside in the sun, and he climbed the basement stairs toward the light.

A few minutes later, Bob joined him and said, "That was Wendy Dean. She remembered that Viki Skalicky moved with her parents to Waite Park shortly after the Benson girl was murdered."

"Where's Waite Park and who the hell is Vicki Skalicky?"

With a sigh, Bob explained that Viki Skalicky was with Benson the day she was murdered. "Skalicky moved to Waite Park the next year and finished

a suburb of St. Cloud and Skalicky had her grades transferred from Gem City High School to St. Cloud Senior High School so she could finish her senior year.

"She could be a person of interest in this case, Dennis. I think we should interview her."

"Okay, the Stearns County Sheriff owes me a favor. It could be arranged."

It was one of Hanson's hyperbolic statements. He neither knew, nor even met Sheriff Jack Neff. Bob was certain Neff didn't owe Hanson any favors.

"Bob do you think this Skalicky had anything to do with Barb Benson's death?"

"I don't know, but she might know something."

"Clear your schedule for tomorrow and we'll interview her."

"Why can't you go by yourself?"

"'Cause it's your case! I'm retired, remember? I'm helping you try to solve it."

It turned out Sheriff Jack did help them out. He offered to have one of his female deputies pick Vicki up and bring her to a conference room at Sheriff's Headquarters.

"Well, Dennis, there's nothing more we can do here. We have no leads. One empty purse, the murder weapon was never found and Dr. Shephard wasn't sure what the hell the weapon actually was. I'm going back to the motel. Tomorrow, we're in St. Cloud."

The long road trip to St. Cloud was unremarkable. The two men took an elevator to the fourth floor where they were ushered in by a female deputy. "Have a seat, gentlemen. Vicki is downstairs. I'll go get her. It's better having her in here instead of a dingy interrogation room."

Vicki Skalicky sat down across from the two cops. She was dark-haired, petite and attractive in a cute sort of way.

Bob Peterson began, "I talked with Wendy Dean. Do you know her? She says you were friends."

"We were friends, but not close."

"Not close? Why?"

"Well, she tried to tag along with the cool kids. She wasn't that cool."

Dennis Hanson jumped in, "Wendy said that you were seen walking with Barbara Benson. The next day, she was murdered."

"I heard she was pregnant. I guess I wanted to console her."

Both men silently agreed that talkative people were more likely to trip themselves up. They hid their smiles.

Peterson: "Were you involved with a John Anderson?"

"Yes, we were going steady for two years. He was a year older."

"I heard you broke up with him when he was getting ready to go to Vietnam."

"He left me."

Peterson's voice rose. "He joined the military! Some guys get married, before they go to war. And some guys get married, if they make it home after a war. That's the way it always was."

"Things were different between us. Besides, he moved to Minneapolis. He still lives there with his parents. I had the sense to move out of my parents' house. I married a wonderful guy. His name is Steve Sullivan. I told him that I was saving myself for marriage. He was so understanding and patient. We've got a three-year-old girl. By the way, I had to leave her with a neighbor.

"Now if you're finished with me, I'd like to go home."

"Dennis, do you have anything you'd like to add?"

"No, not really."

"Vicki, if we need anything more, we'll be in touch."

They began driving back in deafening silence.

Finally, Dennis said, "That was a waste of time. She told us everything and nothing. I wonder what Ed Benson was trying to tell me. Why did Stella kill him?"

"And we, Dennis, should've taken her alive. Then we might have known the answer. Too late, now." He marked the Benson file "COLD" and went home to take the rest of the day off.

That evening, Bob enjoyed the first restful night he had had in the past four years.

The next morning, he looked in the mirror and decided not to shave. He decided not to go to work. Paraphrasing Chief Joseph, he said to himself and then aloud, liking the sound of it, "I shall work no more, forever." It was only a retirement job, he reasoned with himself, and a trivial one at that. He phoned in his resignation to Pinkerton's a few minutes later.

Over the next several years, he made trips to Duluth in the summertime, and sometimes, Thunder Bay. He and his wife Ruthie took the Interstate Highway and never thought to look in Gem City's direction.

Part IV

24. I Was Born ...

I was born at the County Hospital in St. Stephen the same year that Jackie Robinson and Larry Doby integrated major league baseball, and a year before George Herman Ruth, The Babe, passed into immortality.

My parents, Frank and Darlene Anderson, drove me home to Gem City to live with Frank and Darlene and my older brother, Anthony—Tony—a week after I took my first breath. I always thought Tony's name sounded exotic, Italian to be exact, though tempered and tamed by having a bland Norwegian last name. I especially didn't like my name because it was so ordinary and colorless. Everybody called me Johnny. When I was fifteen, I stopped answering and my family thought I'd been struck deaf.

My dad was pretty well-known in Gem City. People would wave to him from across Main Street and yell, "Hey Frankie!" or, "How they hangin,' Andy?" When I heard the name Andy, I thought they were talking about somebody else. But no, they meant Frank. He'd smile and wave back, then mumble under his breath so only I could hear, "Aw, kiss my ass!"

One spring day, when I was about eight, my mother made me go to the National Tea supermarket with her. We were standing there, getting our groceries bagged, when she tapped me on the shoulder and whispered, "That's Earl Swenson," and darted her eyes in his direction. I glanced at him. He was wearing a black wool cap pulled down to his eyebrows. I watched in momentary fascination as his wire-rimmed glasses inched farther down his long, thin nose. When they slid down as far as his nostrils, he pushed them back up. He repeated this four times while I was looking at him. His pale blue eyes stared at nothing in particular.

Earl was a large man and his long, dark coat made him look even bigger. He had a full, blond-gray beard. And he had the largest, reddest, weather-beaten hands I'd ever seen. He alternately and repeatedly jammed those hands deep into his pockets, then took them out and rubbed them. I could hear the sound they made, scraping together like sandpaper on a piece of rough pine. He didn't look at me or anyone else in the store. He just stood and waited impatiently, for his groceries to be bagged. Earl scooped up the bags and hurried to his pickup truck.

So that's Earl Swenson. Well, what about him? I thought. I asked my mom, "Is that man somebody important?"

Mom huffed dismissively, "Why don't you ask your father?"

Ten years later, I finally asked him.

25. Earl Swenson's Story

My dad lit a cigarette, inhaled deeply, pulled a glass ashtray closer and dropped the spent match. He was deep in thought, and I had to wait until he crushed out the butt to tell me the story of Earl Swenson. It began in the 1920s when Gem City was mostly a farming community. Earl, a Norwegian bachelor farmer, sharecropped on the Lewis farm back then.

He was a young, blond, handsome man, and he went to all the barn dances and church socials, though he never became a member of any church. The Norwegian girls of Gem City would giggle nervously whenever they saw him because it was rumored that he was hung like an elk and therefore would probably make a fine husband.

"The guy was fuckin' nuts!" my dad emphasized. "His farmhouse was only one room and it didn't have electricity, indoor plumbing, or a telephone. He did his cooking on a woodstove. I grew up hearing stories about that goddam hermit. Mostly they were rumors told by other kids. One story was pretty consistent—Earl hung around the National Tea for the sole purpose of kidnapping children who strayed from their mothers. He'd stuff them into a gunny sack and take them home to feed his dogs."

Dad kept talking without seeming to take a breath. "Some of the best stories I heard, came from my uncle George Johnson, my mother's sister's husband. George was a Gem City cop for many years. He'd been sent to investigate the disappearance of ten-year old Ira Shifski, and Swenson was the chief suspect in the alleged abduction. Well, turned out the Shifskis' had eight kids and evidently forgot they had sent Ira to Bible Camp for two weeks.

"Late winter that year, I think it was in '55, some of the other farmers reported that they hadn't seen Swenson outside plowing with his team of mules, Maggie and Jiggs. If people didn't see Earl, they could usually hear him geeing and hawing after the mules. But when Earl didn't drive into town that February to buy more feed, people started becoming concerned. The police were called to check on him."

"So, they found him dead?" I asked.

"Did you hear this story before?"

"No, I just figured."

"Yeah, they found him dead. Frozen to death. Stiff as a dried hunka lutefisk! The kids' version of Earl the Monster changed over the years after he died. He became a ghost who stalked the National Tea parking lot looking for children to eat."

26. Tim Wise

Tim Wise and I had been friends and neighbors since he was seven and I was six. He once confided that he was Polish. Somebody, whether it was an immigration agent at Ellis Island or some ancient relative, had shortened and Anglicized the name. His name used to be "Wisnewski." I often greeted him by asking, "What's new, ski?" He only tolerated it for a short time, but by then news of his name had already spread through the grapevine at school. He blamed me for being the grape, which I always denied.

We palled around while we were in high school and spent most summer weekend afternoons and most summer weeknights watching baseball at Parks Field. Though neither of us ever played there, we were in awe of the local celebrities who did.

I felt sorry for Tim because he never saw any baseball games outside of Gem City, except on TV. His family never went anyplace. Even if his dad had a three-week vacation, they spent it within the confines of Gem City. Old man Wise would find some project to get involved with, like painting their house. My family, however, was a little more mobile and never missed a chance to leave town.

When the Minnesota Twins arrived in 1961, we attended the games almost as often as we went to see the Minneapolis Millers. If my mother didn't want to go, we'd drop her off at Southdale. It was out of the way, which always irked my dad. My brother Tony sometimes asked to be dropped-off in downtown Minneapolis. I thought it was because he wanted to watch skin flicks at the Astor Fine Arts Theatre on Fourth and Hennepin. That, instead of baseball? Later, I found out that was exactly what he was doing. I told him he was crazy. Later, I understood.

It was in July one year, in the middle of the week, that I invited Tim Wise to come with me to a Twins day game. With no one to give us a ride, it meant we'd have to take the train to Minneapolis then catch a bus to Metropolitan Stadium. In what was a common summertime ritual, we both begged our dads for some extra money for the train and tickets to the game. Tim's dad gave him the price of a bleacher seat—three bucks. I had to pay an additional five bucks, so we could sit in box seats for a better view.

The Twins were playing the Cleveland Indians and, big surprise, the Twins won. We got to see Harmon Killebrew tag one high and deep to left center. We talked about that game all the way back to Gem City, and for a few weeks afterward.

In those days, I was kind of a practical joker. Tim knew that I often went to the Met and he also knew that it was a goal of mine to see every team in the American League play the Twins. So, I devised the most brilliantly evil hoax I've ever perpetrated. It even surpassed the rubber pencil gag I pulled on Tony. That was bush league compared to this. Tim was sort of a bully and liked to push me, order me around and make lame attempts to trick me.

I had baseball cards, and the 1956 card for that year's series, with players' autographs printed across the bottoms of the cards. All I had to do was trace the signatures and compile them in a bogus autograph book. I used ballpoint pens in black, blue and red ink so that it would look like they were signed at different times. Presto, I had all the names of the big American League stars in a spiral notebook.

In March, on Tim's birthday, I sent him the phony autograph book. Tim was so overcome he nearly fainted. He managed a choked-up, "Thanks man. This is the best birthday present I ever got!"

I watched him go into his house and then I laughed all the way home. A few minutes later though I felt like two cents. But, for fear I'd get my ass pounded, I never told him the truth, and as far as I knew, he never figured it out.

27. Taps for the *Bugle*

I came into the house one day and my dad was grumbling, as usual. Hesitant, but curious, I asked him, "Something wrong?"

Dad rattled the newspaper and shouted, "It's this Gem City *Bugle*! Says this'll be the last issue. It's gonna be bought-out by the St. Stephen *Bulletin*."

Mother had no comment—she just shook her head. She liked to read the death notices in the *Bugle*. You knew when she was reading them because she would suddenly gasp and say things like, "Oh no, Helen Stubbins died!"

And my dad would ask, "Who the hell is Helen Stubbins?"

"Helen was April Johnson's great-aunt."

My dad would just reply, "Oh," and roll his eyes.

I never thought that old man Kelly would sell the *Bugle*, but times being the way they were with circulation hitting rock bottom and Gem City becoming a ghost town almost, he had no other choice. Morris Kelly had purchased the *Bugle* decades earlier when it was only a four-page shopper with advertising on the back. Kelly added three more pages and created the major news source, the pulse of Gem City.

Everyone in town knew the story of why Kelly preferred the term, "death notices" to "obituaries." He had hired an ancient curmudgeon linotype operator named Lewis. Once, before an edition was to run, Kelly admonished Lewis for drinking on the job. In a fit of drunken rage, Lewis set the type that issue by adding an extra "ch" in the middle of "obitchuaries."

The next day, Kelly calmly asked Lewis to teach him how to operate the linotype. Then he fired Lewis. To avoid further misspellings, "Obituaries" became "Death Notices." Ordinary deaths were published as death notices; murders and other unnatural deaths made the front page along with other abnormal stories.

Mayor Felix Nelson made the front page, as did Earl Swenson. Only one of my ancestors made the front page. In fact, he was my mom's great-uncle, Julius, who in 1905 murdered a pitchfork salesman with one of the sample pitchforks. Julius was sent to

Stillwater State Prison to await execution. The following year, when the day had come, Julius was transported to the basement of the Ramsey County Courthouse in St. Paul.

Great-uncle bravely climbed the thirteen wooden steps to the scaffold. The warden asked him if he had any last words. Julius always admired what Nathan Hale had said when he was captured and hanged by the British, so he repeated the patriot's famous last words, "I regret that I have but one life to give for my country."

"Do want us to hang you twice?" the warden laughed.

The hangman tightened the noose around great-uncle's neck, pulled a lever and Julius fell through the trapdoor, his narrow frame jittering in the darkness. The rope stretched, so did great-uncle's neck until poor Julius was standing nearly flatfooted on the floor. The warden was furious because that was the second botched hanging in a year. He asked newspaper reporters to stay silent on hangings that failed to kill in first try, but the news leaked out. Subsequently, capital punishment in Minnesota, was repealed.

28. The Demise of Tim Wise

Tim Wise and I decided that to avoid the military draft after high school by enlisting. I chose the Air Force, and against my advice, Tim joined the Marines. After boot camp, Tim was promptly sent to Vietnam as cannon fodder. We were over there at the same time, Tim in Da Nang and I at Ton Son Nhut airbase. He saw a lot of combat while I saw very little. I worked at the post office.

There was one time when my base was shelled, aiming for the flight line from three miles away but they were way off and hit the mess hall, which in my mind was no big loss.

Tim was still in in Vietnam a month after I'd been stationed back in the States. The Wise family had moved to Northeast Minneapolis, just as my family had done. Tim's dad landed a job driving a moving truck, while my dad got a job at Northern Ordinance.

Then tragedy struck the Wise family. Tim's mother, Ann, who kept contact with my mother, phoned her on a winter weekend with the news. Ann had gotten a visit from a Navy Chaplain and another Marine officer to tell her that Lance Corporal Timothy C. Wise had been killed in Vietnam. Ann said the two men waited while she collapsed onto the sofa.

"How did he die?" she wailed.

"It wasn't combat related," the Chaplain explained. "Your son was assigned to the motor pool where he had been doing some maintenance of a half-ton truck. Apparently, while he was working on the truck he was also working on a bottle of Jim Beam. He decided to take the truck out for a road test. He missed a curve in the road and flipped over. The bottle was found in the wreckage. That's all we know, Mrs. Wise. His body will be prepared and flown to the Naval Air Station out by the airport."

I attended Tim's reviewal, but not his funeral, which was planned for the next morning. The mortuary parking lot had only a few cars in it when I arrived. Inside, a few strangers and vaguely familiar faces milled around in a narrow hallway whispering while I brushed past them unnoticed. A handful of mourners sat on folding chairs in front of the casket. I guessed that the Wises' expected a larger crowd because there were quite a few empty chairs.

Tim's fiancée sat in the front row, Lena, an attractive brunette in a bad mood. Next to Lena sat Tim's sister, Joyce, and Tim's dad, Charlie. Tim's mom posted herself at the foot of the casket, where she greeted people. I smiled politely and shook hands first with Ann then with fiancée and family in the front row. Then I got a cup of watered-down coffee and began milling around with the rest of the peripheral friends and relatives. I could tell which people were aunts, uncles and cousins. Like Charlie, Joyce and Tim, they all had the familial Wise look, prominent noses and underbites.

I finally summoned the courage to walk past Ann to view the bronze-colored casket. There he was, Tim Wise, all spiffed-up in a green Marine dress uniform, a white sidewall haircut, thick makeup slathered on his face. It looked like it had been applied with a push broom. A string of rosary beads were wrapped around his dehydrated, wrinkled hands.

I've always wondered why people say, "He looks so natural," or, "He looks just like he's sleeping," when in fact he looks dead, because he is dead.

I nearly fell backwards when I saw, pinned to the satin lining of the coffin lid, a small notebook. I recognized the scrawl on the cover as my own: "AUTOGRAPHS OF BASEBALL PLAYERS." I began sweating profusely and clapped a hand over my mouth so I wouldn't scream. My face was so wet that it looked like I was overcome with grief, crying. Actually, I was overcome with guilt and almost crying.

I felt an arm drape across my shoulder, causing me to shudder. It was Tim's mother. I gave her a hug and all I could say was, "I'm sorry, I'm sorry," while staring at that stupid autograph book.

She said, "I know."

She had no idea what I was really sorry about.

"Tim told me," Ann whispered, "how much he cherished that autograph book, so I thought I'd send it with him."

Of course, this made me feel worse. I started having bizarre thoughts about that autograph book. Did he ever figure out that I had tricked him? What if he had figured it out and didn't tell me he knew. Then, the last laugh would be his and the joke would be on me. Right? Right?

Whenever I think about it now, the memory torments me. Even if he hadn't figured it out, the joke is still on me!

If there hadn't been an idiotic war in that shitty country, Tim and I would've shared a square bottle and laughed about that joke in our old age; after he soundly kicked my ass, that is.

29. Mick, Judy, Gail and I

A las, poor Mick. It was in the Spring of 1972 that drugs, alcohol and the abuse thereof bought my friend Mick a one-way ticket to the psych unit at the V.A. Hospital. In a rare, lucid moment, before his committal, Mick told me that the Navy made him nuts. I didn't doubt him because he did two harrowing tours in Vietnam during the war. He was a gunner on a Swift Boat in the Lower Mekong Delta on the Bay Hap River.

I visited him at the V.A. a few times, but all the bad, mind-bending acid trips left him totally out of touch with reality and a complete idiot with a bent mind. I could no longer have a normal conversation with him. No one could. That semester, I changed my major to Psychology with a minor in Political Science.

Judy Zelinski and I were headed for a breakup because her husband started getting suspicious. The professor had been working late one night at his office on campus, so I stopped at Judy's house for a couple of hours. When he came home, I was still there.

Judy called to him, "I'm tutoring a student dear."

He headed straight to the bathroom.

The next thing we heard was Zelenski yelling. "Hey, both of you, come in here at once!" Guilt had us by our throats. "There's a condom floating in the toilet!" he bellowed like a wounded walrus.

Judy and I hurried in, looked into the toilet, and Judy said, "What condom?"

I stammered, "Yeah, w-what c-condom?"

"Well," he replied, "it was here." It turned out, after taking a piss, he flushed and the toilet swallowed it. It's a good thing that he's a creature of habit. Judy was thinking the same thing.

(As God is my witness, I swore I flushed that condom, but it was one of those ribbed jobs with a reservoir tip. Sometimes those things get air in them and pop back up.) It was too close a call, so Judy and I split up at the end of Spring semester.

Meanwhile, things were getting hot on campus. Quite a few students decided to go on strike and declared the U of M a to be a "Red University" in protest of the seemingly endless Vietnam War. The University apparently was a huge supporter of the war, especially with the ROTC on campus.

There was every recalcitrant student that a boy from Gem City could imagine, and they weren't members of the audio-visual club or the glee club; they were the hard, angry faces of the SDS, SMC, SWP and its child, the YSA. All left-wingers except for the YAF, a group of right-wing, self-anointed do-gooders. They got harassed each and every day until they disbanded.

There were other groups advising students on how to avoid the draft. Among them were the Quakers, who encouraged conscientious objection and instructed their clients to rehearse sincerity. The Quakers have a long association with objecting to military service, especially during a war. Our president, Richard Milhous Nixon was a Quaker.

With all this activity on campus, there were students, including myself, who only wanted to go to school and get it over with. But I didn't mind seeing democracy in action.

I met one young woman—a cute redhead—and introduced myself.

"Hi, my name's John. What's yours?"

"Why do you wanna know? You writing a book, or something?"

"Well, no. I just wanted to ask you if you want to go with me to the antiwar rally at the Capitol this afternoon. The governor's going to talk to the crowd."

"Look, John, I paid good money to go to school here and it's important to me that I finish my education. So, all these war protesters and the U shutting down and shit, are fucking it up for me!"

"How articulate! But what if, let's say, your boyfriend or your brother were fighting in Vietnam and came home in a box? Then, how would you feel about the war?"

"What time's the rally?"

"At noon. By the way, I gave you my name, what's yours?"

"Gail, that's all. No last names, if you don't mind."

"I think we should take the bus, Gail, otherwise we'll never find a place to park."

"Do you live in a dorm, John?"

"No, I'm staying with my parents. They moved down here and bought a house in Northeast."

"Where did they move from?"

"Gem City."

"Where the hell's that?"

"About a hundred miles Northwest. I was born and raised there."

"I thought it was out-state because you talk funny."

"And where are you from?"

"Anoka."

I stifled a laugh.

We boarded the bus and headed east on University Avenue into St. Paul. Gail was quiet, at first, then she looked at me and caught me staring at her.

"What?"

"Oh, nothing. I was just wondering why you thought I talked funny."

"Because you have such correct grammar. Who'd you have for English?"

"Mrs. Zelinski. Got an A too." I said, proudly.

"Was Zelinski pretty easy?"

I could hardly keep from laughing. My definition of "easy" was radically different than hers.

Not the Governor, but the Lieutenant Governor, Rudy Perpich, came out on the capitol steps and spoke to a crowd of about three hundred for only a few minutes. I was disappointed that we didn't get to see the Governor, but Gail seemed impressed. We got back on the bus to the campus. "You know, John, I should be against the war, too. I have a girl cousin, a lieutenant in the Army. She's a nurse in a mobile hospital in Vietnam. And my dad was in Europe during World War Two. He was wounded pretty bad. He has a lot of trouble bending over and tying his shoes."

30. Back to the Promised Land

Not long after my fling with Gail, I packed a suitcase and headed the one-hundred miles or so northwest to Gem City. The 1970 tornado had leveled a couple of motels, I checked-in to a mom-and-pop motel near St. Stephen. I rolled into Gem City at about four in the afternoon on Friday and stopped at Gene's Standard. Most people stop there first when they're coming up from the south. When Gene saw me pull in, he came bounding out to pump the gas. I said, "Ten bucks worth of regular."

He stared at me for a moment, then asked, "I feel like I should know you. Who the hell are you?"

"Orson Welles," I said, trying to be funny.

"No, you're too young. Hey, I know, you're John Anderson. Wow, it's been a long time, John! How've you been? Where've you been?"

"I graduated high school and went in the Air Force. Now I'm at the U So, what's up with you, Gene?"

"I'm the mayor again; Natalie's on the council and Wendy was on it too but went back to St. Cloud. We didn't bother to hold a special election. The people left here only vote for presidential candidates, anyway. Say, who do ya think's gonna win? Nixon or McGovern?"

"I really don't know, Gene."

"All I know, John, if it was up to Gem City, McGovern will be in the White House, come January."

"How many people are left after the tornado?"

"Oh, I'd say about sixteen-hundred."

Gene put gas in my car, checked the oil and cleaned the windshield. I told him that I was going to look around town a little before going to visit Johnny Briggs, the cemetery caretaker.

"That old Johnny Briggs," Gene said, "he'll probably live long enough to bury me."

I drove past the decaying, Nesterud Memorial Library and made my way to the former Parks Field. For me and a lot of others, that ballfield was sacred ground, and some idiot had to come along and build townhouses. Pure sacrilege. I felt that Parks Field was meting out justice because most of the townhouses built there, had either fallen down or sank into the soft landfill. But what memories that sacred ground held!

Memories cascaded over me. There were ballgames played which could truly be called, great.

31. Mr. Briggs

I turned off Main Street onto the short gravel road and through the wrought iron gate of Gethsemane Cemetery. The gate stood open, but lopsided, perhaps owing to the tornado. There was no fence around the graveyard, just half-dead arborvitae surrounding the property, those that the tornado hadn't toppled.

A rail-thin black man stepped out of the granite building that served as an office and living quarters for Johnny Briggs, the caretaker. He wore a white shirt, the long sleeves rolled up to his elbows, top button buttoned at his throat. A pair of gray suspenders held up his loose-fitting blue jeans.

I hollered, "Mr. Briggs, Johnny, how're you doing?"

He squinted through wire-rimmed glasses and asked, "Who the hell are you?"

"John Anderson. Remember me? The last time we saw each other was about ten years ago. You put some of my people to rest here; the Andersons, Olsons, Thompsons."

"Yeah, I vaguely remember you. At first I thought you were just a tourist. You know, come to visit the graves of Gem City's famous and infamous."

Johnny looked only slightly different since the last time I saw him., more bent over, and his hair, what little of it he had left, had turned wispy and completely white. His hair reminded me of a dandelion gone to seed.

"Yeah," he said, "most folks who come here want to look at the Benson family plot. They were somthin' else, that bunch. All three were killed and buried within a week. I couldn't even come out of the office when they lowered poor Barbara Benson."

Briggs asked me where I was when all of this happened. I told him I was in Vietnam and my girlfriend at the time, was a classmate of Barb Benson. She wrote me a letter telling me about the funeral and how ghastly it was. All the letters she wrote me were "Dear John" letters, but the last one turned out to be a real Dear John. Would've served her right if I'd come home in a box. We'd talked about getting married when I came home on leave for Christ's sake, but it wouldn't have worked out anyway because she was Catholic. My dad told me that mixed marriages between Catholics and

Lutherans are always doomed to failure. Plus, he was convinced that marrying out of my nationality was a sin and marrying out of my religion was even worse. My mother agreed."

"You best off free to play the field, John."

"Well, I am playing. Say, Johnny, earlier I talked with Gene Dean and …"

"That fuckin' crook? You actually had an intelligent conversation with him?"

"Why do you call him a crook?"

"Well, do you remember the '65 tornado? Mr. Dean got us the federal disaster money all right but kept a lot of it for himself."

"How could he do that?"

"Because some people just abandoned their houses and never came back. He had close to a million bucks. He was and still is able to pay himself sixty-eight G's a year. Whenever his wife is mayor, he pays her the same, while he takes a cut of forty thousand.

"Then, after the '70 tornadoes, there was more federal money for Gene Dean because more people left and very few demanded money to re-build their homes."

"Do people know this?"

"I don't know if everybody does."

"Why don't you run for mayor or city council? Maybe you could stop some of this chicanery."

"I was on the city council, two terms with Gene's daughter Wendy. Me and her got along just fine and were sometimes able to keep Gene under control."

"Wow, I didn't realize he was that way. At least he stopped doing his James Dean routine. He seemed completely obsessed with old J.D."

"He still is, man. And when he's drinkin' it's worse. He'll start screaming, 'Why can't any of you understand?' and it scares people away. Yeah, he's nuts.

"One time, he challenged me to a chicken race like they did in *Rebel Without a Cause*. There's a cliff by the river … we were supposed to drive as close to the edge as we could, before we could jump out and the cars wound up in the river. The first one who jumps is a chicken. I did not want to send my brand-new Lincoln over a cliff and into the goddam river. Period."

"You drive a Lincoln? I never imagined that Gem City paid you that kind of money."

"Haven't you heard? The county bought Gethsemane—that's more money for Mayor Dean and me, of course. For an easy job, it pays pretty good."

"Where did you work before?"

"Oh, that's a story for another time. Wait a minute, there might not be another time because I feel that my earthly time'll be up soon. My bones ache, I cough a lot and the cords in my neck stick out. Now, if that's not a sign, I don't know what is. So, I'd better go ahead and tell the story before I get any older. Besides, you asked for it.

"I was workin' at the Hotel Metropolitan in Chicago as an elevator operator. They had me all dressed up in a maroon uniform with brass buttons and gold braid around my shoulder. I looked like a fuckin' general. Anyways, I was waiting for someone to get on, when in walks this beautiful, and I mean, gorgeous, young, Negro lady. She had caramel-colored skin … high yellow we called it, and one of those summery dresses made of light material that swished when she walked. She had on a white hat as wide as her shoulders, and she smelled like a bouquet of flowers. Then, she said real soft-like, 'Four, please.' It wasn't what she said, it was how she said it. She kinda purred it. She coulda knocked me right over. I could feel myself fallin'. I went over to the desk and peeked at the registry. She was Mrs. Charlotte Hendricks of Cicero, Illinois. Missus? The letters jumped off the page … MRS.? I was so confused and disappointed. I didn't know what to think. I seen her in the lobby a number of times, comin' and goin' as she pleased, head held high. Shit, I wouldn't've been allowed near that woman if I wasn't the elevator man. I found out that she was stayin' for three days only. I had to work fast. I couldn't let her leave without talkin' to her. Then I got my chance. She was about to get on the elevator when I asked, 'It's time for my break. Could I buy you a cuppa coffee?' And she said, 'I don't know why not.' Well, talking to her, some interestin' things came to light. See, Charotte, that was her name, she used the Mrs. when travelin' … came downtown Chicago to meet with her stockbroker. Turns out she was a widow, and she was loaded to the hilt. Her husband was killed in the World War. She also got a ton of money from her daddy who invented the bastard file, or somethin'."

"Johnny, I hate to interrupt, but how long a story is this?"

Johnny laughed. The sun reflected off the gold sliver between his front teeth. "It'll end soon. The following month we were married in Cicero. You know, I still can't figure out why she picked me of all people. I'm a homely mug and, man, she was beautiful! I quit my stupid job and lived with her in the prettiest house I ever saw. It was a red brick colonial with white trim. There was a grand piano in the parlor, five bedrooms upstairs, a fully stocked library and a telephone in every damn room. We were sitting pretty till the Crash came, and the Depression. By then, we were both so ass-deep in debt we no choice but to become bootleggers. We had made the acquaintance of a couple of shiners and went into business as distributors of their product. Long story short, Charlotte was in the middle of a morning moonshine run when her car conked out on the railroad tracks. The Empire Builder what got my Charlotte in the end. I got depressed. Sold the house. Not long afterward I heard that real bootleggers, and real gangsters were lookin' for me 'cuz they believed I owed them money. Some shit like that. I packed up moved to Gem City."

"Why here, Johnny? You had to know you'd stand out."

"I thought so too at first. But there was a few black families here and they would've warned me if some strangers came to town askin' about me. Then I'da hightailed it. Yeah, been here thirty years and I'm not going anyplace else … even after I'm dead. I got a my plot right over there by the corner of the building."

Briggs gestured toward his final resting place then, swept his hand across the entire cemetery and announced, "I am the sentinel, the guardian of the subterranean and the shepherd of the people who lie here. Why shouldn't I want to stay with them?"

He must have noticed the startled look on my face because he smiled and said, matter-of-factly, "We all wind up here sooner or later, John. I spoze you probably think it's scary that I live here. But you know what? You don't have to be afraid of dead people, son. They won't hurt you. It's only the live ones who do the hurtin'."

"Yeah, I do know that."

"So, how're your folks, John? They still in Minneapolis? Are they ever comin' back?"

"Fine, yes and no. Anyway, Mr. Briggs, I hate to see what's

happened to this town. I mean, you can see that it's dying."

"Son, that's where you are very wrong. Gem City's had a little setback, that's all. Don't you read the *Bugle*? Now it's called the *Bulletin*. Well, don't you read it?"

I just nodded and said, "When I lived here I read the *Bugle*. Why?"

"Because Gem City's gonna be annexed by St. Stephen is why. We get to keep our name, and we get to keep our mayor and council. The thirty-mile stretch between us'll be lined with big restaurants, hotels, a county museum and a Target store."

"You're shitting me."

"Not shitting you. Mayor Dean condemned some of the bigger houses left behind and is gonna turn 'em into Bed and Breakfasts. There'll be antique shops, a couple of chain restaurants disguised as mom-and-pop cafes."

"Tell me Johnny, do you that plan'll work?"

"Young man, you just hafta have faith. Sometimes, you hafta to go with the flow and work with the crooks like Gene Dean. And, if it works, it'll save Gem City. Why, it should bring in tourists. Maybe our former residents'll move back. The welcome signs'll change to say, 'Stay for a while in Historic Gem City.' Oh that'll bring people here, for sure."

"I hope you're right."

"Man, got to be. Well sir," he said, indicating our conversation had concluded, "I've got to go inside and watch the news while I have lunch. What're you gonna do now?"

"I'm gonna drive around town. I'm staying one more night in St. Stephen before heading back to Minneapolis."

"Hey John, before you go, I'll show you some shit I collected over the years." He opened a drawer in his desk. "People actually leave this stuff, plastic flowers, toys, dolls, teddy bears ... and here's one ... found this dangling on the brass railing and quick grabbed it before it fell in the grave. It's a bracelet." He handed it to me. I concealed my surprise—no raised eyebrows—turning it over, in my hand, I saw the smaller the smaller inscription on the underside, "John." *Vicki was at Barb's burial!*

I'd had her name inscribed in script lettering on polished steel. I remember she was thrilled, overjoyed. I told her I was going to be shipped to Nam in about a month and hoped that she'd be wearing it when and if I came back home.

"Vicki, it looks a little big for you. I can get a link taken out."

"No, John, I like it this way." She turned it on her wrist, raised her hand and let it slide up her arm.

"Oh John, you know what? I'm gonna take you to dinner. I'll buy."

She meant her dad would buy. He had rules; if she went on a date and it was a school night, She'd have to be home at nine p.m., providing she had her homework done. On weekends, she could stay out until ten, if her homework was done for Monday.

That September, after I completed boot camp, I came home on leave for thirty-days. This afforded me the opportunity to do whatever I wanted, late at night. Barbara Benson was available and I reasoned, if Vicki wouldn't "put-out," maybe Barb would.

Dates with Vicki were movies or dinner. After that, I'd pick Barb up after work at the Qik Stop. She called her dad; told him she already had a ride home.

After the first of several nights in a motel, I was getting my due of "goodbye sex." It surprised me that she seemed adequately experienced ... actually, more than I was.

Johnny turned to go back to the office, then spun around and said, "Listen, don't be a stranger. Come back and visit as often as you want."

"Yes, I intend to." I started walking to my car.

"One more thing, John. Always treat people with sincerity, but also remember the warning of Oscar Wilde who said, 'A little sincerity is a dangerous thing and a great deal of it is absolutely fatal.'"

I returned his wave goodbye and said, over my shoulder, "Okay Johnny, I'll remember."

32. The End of Gem City?

I continued my drive through what remained of Gem City wanting to find out who survived and stayed and who didn't. On the way to my former home, my first stop was my first ex-girlfriend's house. Only the foundation remained. I momentarily hoped she was in it when the tornado hit. *Forget it, will ya? The thing's been over for years. But, no matter what, bitch, I'll get even! If the Gem City* BUGLE *and the Minneapolis* STARTRIBUNE *published personal ads, certainly the Saint Cloud* TIMES *did the same. Vicki, more than likely, found her "Mister Right" among those personals. Following that line of logic, I placed the following ad in the Times:*

"Dear Vicki, I know what you did, why you did it and will never let you get away with it. John."

Next, I pulled up in front of the vacant Joel Penn Elementary School. Memories, good and bad, swept through my consciousness like a hoard of locusts. One of the things I remembered quite vividly was a bully named Everett Barnes. God, if someone had just killed him. In fact, a group of boys attacked Everett one time after school and hoping to do just that, but he beat the hell out of all six of them.

Everett was a bully up until the ninth grade, which is when he ran into upperclassmen in high school. Everette's bully career was almost over. I may have helped end it.

It's a well-known fact that bullies make terrible athletes. We were in sophomore gym class. It was a warm fall day, so the class played a game of touch football outside. I wasn't too big back then, but nevertheless, I was on the high school football team. Unfortunately for Everette, he was lined up on offense for the opposing team directly across from me. My assignment was to run in and tag their quarterback before he threw the ball. Everett was the only obstacle standing in my way.

I did the old hit and spin-off maneuver and caught him in the ear with my elbow. He fell down bellowing. The gym teacher thought at the time that poor Everette had a concussion, but it turned out that he just had a very bad headache for a couple of days. It took the same amount of time for his hearing to come back.

Being a baseball fanatic, I wanted to play baseball in high school but had to accept second best, the goddam football team. In some sort of rebellion, I chose Mickey Mantle's number seven. My jersey must've previously been worn by a much taller kid because the bottom of the number was tucked into my pants, making it look like a number one.

My position was tailback in the standard I-formation. I'd always thought I was a mediocre football player, but in comparison to my teammates I was a star. In my senior year, we were tied for last place with St. Stephen until we played them. We won that game, probably because they wanted to lose more than we did.

Breaking from my reverie, I drove over and stopped at the curb in front of the Benson house, standing intact, and vacant, with an orange condemned sign nailed to the door. *That thing should be bulldozed.* I a short time, the Benson family was wiped out. Ed and Barbara, murdered; Stella Benson chose suicide by cop. Stories circulated that the police pumped so much lead into her that she'd gained twenty pounds. Yet, it was only one of the worst things that occurred in Gem City's history.

I arrived at my former home on Washington Street. It was still standing minus a few shingles and some second-floor windows were broken. There was no condemned sign on the front door. I got out and tried the front door. Of course, it was locked. So I broke a window and crawled in. To my surprise, it was in pretty good shape except it was dirty and devoid of furnishings. Would it be out of the question if I took the house back and lived here again? I lit a cigarette and the thought vanished as quickly as it came.

I went outside to the large backyard, where Tony and I used to play catch with a baseball green from tossing each other grounders. Even though I was only in seventh grade, I was obsessed with the idea that someday I'd pitch for the city team, the Gems, then, following that glorious career, go on the pitch for the New York Yankees.

One sunny Spring day, Tony and I were playing catch, when I decided to practice pitching. I'd been working on a circle-curve. My dad was bent over pulling dandelions with a pronged sticker, not paying attention to us. Well, I lost control of my circle-curve and hit him in the side of the head. He didn't see it coming. The ball made a curious sound, like a hammer hitting a hollow tree.

For some reason, Dad's reflexes told him to wheel around and throw the dandelion sticker at Tony who adeptly jumped out of the way. The sticker hit the wooden fence and stuck there, vibrating. Tony and I took off in different directions and didn't come back till nightfall. By the time we got home, my mother had somehow mellowed out my dad. Years later, she informed me that she told him not to kill us because he had to go to work the next morning.

33. Change, Good or Bad, Is Just Change.

Why the hell did I have to come back here? Following the tornadoes, people ran away from Gem City in droves. What was it about this town that called me back? I suppose I'll never figure it out.

Walking back to my car from my childhood home I saw the now familiar sign on my former neighbors, the Wises' door. It read: NO TRESPASSING. THIS PROPERTY IS CONDEMNED BY ORDER OF THE MAYOR OF GEM CITY. There was no such notice on my house, and I found it odd my house had been spared condemnation.

I wanted to drive the entire length of Main Street before heading out to the highway. I didn't know if I'd ever see Gem City again. If I did come back, it would be to fight and try to put an end to Mayor Dean's hegemonic oligarchy. There'd certainly be hell to pay.

I stopped in front of a vacant lot, the stubble of a building foundation. The movie theater once proudly stood there. The city used the refuse from demolishing the building to fill a nearby swamp. I still miss that old Ruby Theater. In 1968, the city condemned it and tore it down. As part of the city's Main Street development plan, a two-story fitness center was going to be built on the same site. At the last minute, the developer backed out and the property was left vacant and remained vacant ever afterward.

In 1955, Al Eckstein, the owner and manager of the Ruby theater, advertised that a real movie star was going to appear, "Live! On Stage!" for a motion picture premier. No movie had ever premiered at the Ruby. Al always boasted about his connections to Hollywood. Everyone knew better.

Saturday matinees for kids, Al showed old westerns, which were in public domain so he didn't have to pay royalties. He did this for years, until people started buying televisions. The same movies played on TV for free.

Ever the entrepreneur, Eckstein, in an effort to boost attendance, actually did get a real movie star to appear—Keye Luke. Mr. Luke introduced a Charlie Chan double feature and talked a little about the film series. He was in the movies as Charlie Chan's number one son. Eckstein was right. The event packed the theater. Luke was the first and last movie star to step onto the stage at the Ruby.

One time, my brother Tony and I were taking a shortcut home and walked behind the theater. Tony clapped his hands to his face and yelled, "Johnny, look at this—goddam!" There it was—never in my wildest dreams—the most popcorn I'd ever seen, all in one place. It was a mountain of manna to a couple of popcorn addicts, such as we. Eckstein had thrown it out the night before. Some of it was burnt, but that was okay. We were chowing down as if we were possessed.

When Eckstein saw us, he came running, screaming, "Hey you kids, don't eat that shit, you'll die!" We grabbed what we both could carry and ran away laughing. In those days, we laughed at death.

After the Ruby was demolished, the only logical alternative was to go to the movies at the Main, a drive-in theater built in the early '50s. It was four blocks from Main Street at the end of town.

Before it opened for the season in 1968, the school district bought the property and tore it down. They told everyone it was for future expansion of the district and that a new middle school would soon be built on the site. Due to declining enrollment, the school was never built and like the Ruby, the Main's property sat vacant forever.

With no movie theater to go to in Gem City, there was no choice, but to drive up to St. Stephen. They had bulldozed their architecturally functional single screen theater and replaced it with a brand new, multi-screen, cinder block concoction which would not look out of place substituting as a bunker in Alamogordo. That thing had seven action-packed screens, but their popcorn tasted like Styrofoam, and upon request, the snack bar kids would pour some yellow oily crap over it. They called it golden topping. Just from the name of it, you knew it wasn't real butter. They poured real butter at the Ruby and the Main.

When The Main was razed, a cry rose up from all the teenagers in Gem City: "Remember The Main!"

34. Poor Dad, Poor Mom, Poor Me.

The drive home to Minneapolis seemed longer than usual. I walked in the door and the unmistakable aroma of meat cooking on the stove made me salivate like Pavlov's dog.

"Just relax, John," my mother said, "supper won't be ready for at least a couple hours. We're having pot roast."

"Dad's favorite," I groused.

Mom stood with her back against the sink, arms akimbo. My dad sat in his usual spot at the head of the kitchen table. An almost full bottle of Jack Daniel sat in front of him. He drained what remained in his juice glass. We had eight of those glasses with rings of oranges painted around the tops. He got up to get me one from the cupboard.

"Ever wonder why," he asked, "the best hooch comes in square bottles?"

I shrugged. "Beats me."

"Because," he answered himself, "if you pass out on a hill, it won't roll away. You want me to pour two fingers?"

"No, thanks. I've already had a long day and besides, I've got an early class tomorrow."

"What's the matter? Too proud to drink with your old man?"

"All right Dad. Just two fingers."

"My fingers or yours?" he asked with a grin. I don't know why the hell he asks me when he measures with his fingers anyway and I'd always wind up with two-and-a-half of the amber stuff.

"Careful with that," my mother warned, "you'll ruin your appetite."

"Hey Dad, what's with the neighbor?"

"What do you mean?"

"He's got a Confederate flag hanging on his living room wall. I never noticed it before, 'cause he always had his curtains pulled shut. Maybe I should go over and tell him that his side lost."

"No you won't. He's got enough troubles being a moron. His wife and kids left him, so he was gonna kill himself, see. He turns on the oven, sets the thing at 450 degrees and stuck his head in. Burned all his hair off, for the Christ sake."

"Geez," I said and poured myself another. "Didn't he know enough to blow out the flame?"

"Of course not," Dad rasped. "And that's not all." He lit a cigarette and smiled at Mom. "The dope came over when I was at work and I guess you were at school. This was about a year ago. Anyway, he came over and tried to hustle your mother."

"How come I never heard any of this before?" I said, glancing over at Mom, who had taken a hand off her hip and put it over her mouth to conceal either a smirk or a yawn. I sat looking at her and tried to imagine if anyone besides my dad, could be attracted to her. She wasn't at all bad looking, in fact she was rather attractive for a middle-aged woman, and of course a middle-aged man might be attracted to her. I turned back to my dad, who was laughing.

"Yeah, John, I had to go next door and flatten his snot locker for him."

"You did what?"

Dad whirled away from the table and stood to demonstrate how he did it. Even though he was in his mid-fifties, he was still a mass of sinew, large, chiseled forearms and biceps. He shuffled his feet and started shadow boxing, his big fists flying at an imaginary idiot.

"I faked with a right hook, he moved his guard, then I nailed him with a straight left jab. Keeyrunch! I heard it crack. He grabbed his nose with both hands and ran back into his house."

"Dad, why didn't you tell me this before?"

'Cause you probably would've tried to stop me, or something. Here's a lesson you young people have to learn, chivalry isn't dead. I revived it with one punch."

"No, I wouldn't've tried to stop you." I looked over at Mom again. She was smiling, beaming at Dad.

Dad staggered back to the table and practically fell into his chair. He hadn't had that much to drink, not yet. He reached for the bottle but I grabbed it first and filled his glass. After a long silence, I finally asked him if something was wrong. Mom pushed herself away from the sink and joined us at the table.

"I had a brain injury years ago and sometimes it comes back to haunt me. I have these little dizzy spells and lose my concentration.

And since I operate a drill press, I worry I could have a spell and drill through one of my fingers."

"How serious is it? And why didn't you tell me about this before? When did it happen?"

"Well, you oughta know."

"What the hell is that supposed to mean?"

"You were playing catch with Tony. I played baseball for damn near twenty years and you're the only guy ever to bean me."

"That had to have been about fifteen years ago. Besides, I was just a kid practicing my pitching."

"You weren't any good at it. You couldn't pitch worth a goddam. You tried out for the high school team and didn't make it as a pitcher, or any other position."

"I was a pretty good hitter, though."

"Yeah, but you gotta be able to catch and throw to play baseball, numbnuts."

"I lettered in football."

"Big deal. You put your head down and ran with the ball. Now, your brother Tony, there was a baseball player. Other than me, he was the best second baseman Gem City ever saw. We've got a closet full of his and my trophies."

"Do you suppose," my mother interjected, "we could change the subject to something more pleasant?"

"But I want to get back to what I was gonna say. Because of these spells, I don't think I can make it to retirement. I'll have to quit my job. If we want to stay here, you or your mother will have to go to work. Maybe both of you. I think it should be you, though."

"You mean, quit school? I've only got a year left, Dad!"

"Oh, you can finish some other time. Maybe I can pull a few strings and they'll hire you at Northern Pump."

"I don't wanna work at the Pump. I'd rather work someplace close by."

"Then try Paper-Calmenson Foundry. They're union."

There was a long silence until Mom spoke. "We heard from Tony. He quit his job as a computer programmer in Silicon Valley and moved to Las Vegas to become a blackjack dealer."

"So," I said, "he left Silicon Valley for Silicone Valley?"

Pretending she didn't hear what I said, Mom continued. "We don't have to worry about Tony. Unlike you, he's always been quite successful at anything he does. Well, anything except marriage. He had to divorce that Cheryl. It was her fault of course. That's how he wound up in Las Vegas. Oh, and there's something else we want to tell you.

"Your dad and I called Johnny Briggs at the cemetery in Gem City and bought three plots there."

"Three plots. Why three?"

Dad answered my question. "The three of us, your mother and me and you. You'll be right between us."

I sprang up from the table. "You did what? How do you know that I don't want to be buried at Fort Snelling National Cemetery? In fact, all of us could be buried there."

"The trouble with being buried in that place," Dad added, "is nobody can find you."

"Hell," I said, "you don't want anybody to find you now!"

"Be that as it may, John, it's a done deal."

"Well, folks, why don't we just move back to Gem City? We still have our house, there."

"No we don't."

"There wasn't any condemned sign on the door."

"It wasn't damaged by the tornado and the city bought it. How do you think we could afford to buy this house, dum-dum?"

35. Yeah, But What About Tony?

The following day, a sad one, I drove to the University's Administration Building to cancel all my classes for the Fall semester, along with my contract parking space. My education would be placed on hold for a time yet to be determined.

I cruised by Stub and Herb's to see if it was open. Thank god, it was. Even though I had the rest of the morning, hell, the rest of the day for a few bumps. It was a gorgeous September day, which I didn't want to waste sitting in a darkened bar, so I only gulped down four whiskey sours before heading home to make an interview appointment at Paper-Calmenson.

On the way there, I saw a small group, I assumed were students, gathered in front of the ROTC Armory, which had always reminded me of a medieval castle. They were confronting some young cadets dressed in olive-drab army fatigues as the men entered the building. I was curious and pulled to the curb behind the students. There were six of them, four women and two men.

They shouted at the cadets, "More training for the baby killers!" The cadets only smiled and waved to the students.

"You don't have to do this, you know," one woman called out. "You're going to die for a country that doesn't care about you!" another added.

During a lull in the shouting, I asked one of the young men why they were protesting. "The war is over."

The young man answered angrily, "They're being trained for the next war in another third world country!"

"Well, if that's true," I said, "I guess you've got a valid point."

"Fuckin'-a-right, we do!" another intoned.

Then they broke into an old Baptist hymn, which at first, seemed to be impromptu, except one of the women blew an E-flat on a pitchpipe. It was *Down by the Riverside.*" I thought it was an appropriate selection for two reasons. The ROTC castle was located, ironically, on Church Street, and the second verse of the hymn fit the occasion.

"I'm gonna lay down my sword and shield / down by the riverside and study war no more."

On the way home, I stopped at Mac and Cap's for a couple more belts. When I got home, I found my dad sitting on the couch watching *Love, American Style*. God, I hated that show.

"Hey, John. C'mere. Guess what?" Dad called before I had both feet inside the house and had a chance to say, what? He said Mom had already gotten a job as a receptionist in a doctor's office.

"Is she home?"

"No, she's out shopping for new outfits. Yeah, she interviewed this morning and starts tomorrow. I guess she never let her typing skills rust. And let that be a lesson to you. Never let your skills rust. Too bad you don't have any skills. ..."

I cut him off with a question. "What about Tony? Is he going to help us out by sending money home?"

"What the hell? Why're you bringing your brother into this? It's only between us, understand? Besides, he's got his own life to worry about."

"It would be better if he just moved back here."

I landed a job at Paper-Calmenson as a grinder, which meant deburring excess material from large hunks of iron, steel and aluminum. All things considered, I would've rather been sitting in a classroom, studying Greek Classics.

On occasion, I'd complain to my dad about the appalling working conditions at my job and he'd always say, "You don't know what appalling is." And leave it there for me to figure out.

A few months flew by and it was winter again. When it was below-zero, the only consolation to working in a foundry was that, for a quick warmup, workers would stand in front of a 4,000-degree furnace. The Safety Department, however, was kind enough to warn us not to carry butane lighters in our pockets, there having been several fatal explosions in the past.

My mother's health started to deteriorate rapidly. She had complained to her boss, the doctor, of chronic stomach pain and sudden weight loss. The doctor offered to give her a complete physical at no cost. After running some tests, the lab results revealed that she had an advanced case of inoperable pancreatic cancer. She didn't tell Dad or me about it until late that winter.

From then on, most of my wages went toward buying cases of Jack Daniel, which I shared with my parents. My mother, who never was much of a drinker, began developing an appetite for sour mash.

36. The Return of Tony

With both my mom's and my wages combined, the total nearly equaled what my dad had been making at Northern Ordnance, and it helped for a while, until Mom got sick and was sent home to rest. I hired a home health aide to help Dad take care of her while I was working. We all had to cut down on our copious consumption of Old Number 7 so I could afford the extra expense. I even phoned Tony and appealed to him for financial help, but he refused, saying that a Blackjack dealer doesn't make much money.

My dad always told me to use my head for "something other than a hat rack." So, I had him co-sign for a new mortgage loan.

My dad sat on the couch in front of the TV, while Mom confined herself to bed, sipping teacups of J.D. and reading the Book of Revelations from the Bible. She reasoned that if the end was near for her, it may also be for the rest of us. Some days, I hoped it was.

On the advice from the home health aide, I had Mom sent to a nursing home where hospice was provided. Dad and I visited her every day when I came home from work. The hospice unit was a quiet, darkened, somber place. The fluorescent light above her bed made her appear even more emaciated and jaundiced than she actually was. I turned it off and let weak sunlight slant into the room from the single window; watched the morphine drip, one drop per six seconds, into her left arm.

She spoke to us. "Frank, John. I have to tell you both," she said, as she stopped staring at the ceiling and looked sadly at Dad and me. "I had a vision last night. It wasn't a dream. It was like watching a movie, but the whole thing lasted a few seconds."

"What was it about?" I asked.

"Don't interrupt," Dad mumbled, "let her tell it."

"It was like seeing the past, present and future, all at the same time. In fact, I saw the beginning of Time itself. Then, I saw my own life, which didn't last very long. In the next scene, the three of you—Tony was there too—were crying beside my grave."

"Could you see anything beyond that, Mom?"

"It was pretty hazy, but I could see you, John. You were standing in Gethsemane Cemetery all by yourself."

Dad only looked at me and shook his head.

"Mom, did this, your vision, have anything to do with your reading Revelations?"

She smiled enigmatically, and simply said, "No. Revelations is not about what you think it's about."

As soon as we got home, Dan and I sat at the kitchen table and began the ritual of talking, smoking and drinking.

"You know Dad, I think what she said back there, was pretty profound."

"And you know what I think? It was the morphine talking."

At 12:45 a.m. on the first Sunday in April, 1975, the hospital called. Mom had passed away. *Passed away? She wasn't driving a car on the highway. Couldn't they say she died?*

I woke Dad and told him that Mom had entered the shadow world of the unknown, except she knew where she was going.

"What? What the hell're you talkin' about? You mean she's dead?" I didn't answer, only nodded. Intense shock, sadness and anger, mostly anger, swept over us. Dad said, "John, you'd better call Tony."

"I'm sure he's still at work."

"Well shit, call him at the Golden Nugget. Do it now. Tell him what happened and tell him that we'll wire him enough for a one-way ticket."

"One-way? Isn't he gonna pay for the return trip?"

"Don't ask questions! Just do what I tell you to do."

After calling Tony, I called a mortuary nearest the nursing home and told them to pick up Mom's body and said I'd call them later to make funeral arrangements.

Neither Dad nor I went back to sleep. We sat and looked at each other. There was nothing to say that hadn't already been said. We chain-smoked cigarettes. I paced myself with the J.D. I didn't want to be drunk when I made phone calls.

Tony's flight was about to arrive. Dad told me to take his car and pick Tony up, because my car was a "dangerous piece of junk" which might make Tony uncomfortable.

I went to the Northwest terminal and met Tony at the gate. Realizing that it had been years since I'd last seen him, I prepared myself to look for an older Tony. I expected what I saw walking from the gangway, a balding, well-tanned, robust man wearing Ban-Ray sunglasses, faded blue-jeans, a western-style denim sport coat over a plain white t-shirt and tan cowboy boots. I could not imagine how I would look to him.

"Hi, John. It's been quite a while."

"Tony, you haven't changed a bit."

We'd always lied to each other and our lies flowed like sewage, downhill, through a large pipe. Tony took off his sunglasses and we gave each other a tight hug. He had that familiar Anderson scent of cigarettes, aftershave and booze. He wore sunglasses to hide swollen eyes.

"God, John, I'm tired. I haven't slept in two days. So, when's Mom's funeral? I'm only here four days."

"I hate to tell you this, but there's not gonna be a funeral or reviewal."

"What? I wanted to see her one more time."

"You wouldn't've wanted to see her, not the way she looked at the end. You've got recent pictures to remember how she used to look. I think you know she's gonna be buried in Gem City."

"Yeah, it's a good place to be buried, both literally and figuratively."

"What're you talking about? There's big plans for Gem City."

"Oh, I know. I still have a subscription to the St. Stephen *Bulletin*. By the way, did you put an obituary notice in that paper?"

"It'll be in next week. It's just gonna say that there was a private, graveside ceremony at Gethsemane presided over by Reverend Erickson from St. Stephen Lutheran Church."

"John, would you drive through town? I wanna see what downtown Minneapolis looks like these days."

"Did you bring any other clothes, or are you going to wear what you've got on, tomorrow?"

"Well, what the hell do you think? I've got a white shirt in the suitcase and a black bowtie from my wedding."

"Shit, Tony. I guess the bowtie is okay, but I hope the shirt's not one of those tuxedo ones with the ruffles."

"No, wiseass, it's not. Aren't we there, yet?"

37. Back to Gem City, Again

When we arrived at the house, I let Tony go in first, so that he and Dad could greet each other without my being too close. My dad was sitting at the kitchen table with his face in his hands, an unopened bottle of Jack Daniel sitting within reach.

"Tony, I knew you'd come!"

"Thanks for sending me the airfare," Tony said. He wrapped his arms around Dad's shoulders. Dad reached up and gently patted Tony on the cheek. I stood at the sink in quiet observation.

"John," Dad called, motioning for me to come closer to the table, "I can't get this goddam bottle open." Before I could reach for it, Tony twisted the cap off. "Tony, get three glasses from the cupboard and pour us each one."

"Dad," I said, "I think we'd better get something to eat first."

"Never you mind, John. We're just gonna have one first."

We went to a restaurant, a nice one, on Lowry and Second Street. With dinner, we each had two Windsor's neat.

Back at the house, we continued drinking Old Number 7 and began reminiscing about my mom. Each time one of us told a story, we'd sob and bawl like newborn Bassett Hounds. It was cathartic though, like a high colonic for our souls.

"In the morning," Dad told Tony and me, "we're gonna follow the hearse to Gem City. I picked out a white one. Black's for boys, white's for girls." I swallowed hard when I thought about the finality of it all.

"Was she embalmed?" Tony asked.

"No," Dad answered, "she's in a closed casket. So, this is the plan for tomorrow, we're gonna leave at 10:00 and follow the hearse and get to the cemetery by 12:30. Of course, we'll be stopping halfway for gas and restrooms."

"Sounds like a plan, Dad," Tony said as he raised a glass of J.D.

"Oh, there's one other thing, Tony."

"What's that, Dad?"

"The Wises' are driving behind us in two cars. Charlie and Ann in one car and Joyce and her girlfriend, Cynthia, in the other."

"What? Why?"

"'Cause, Tony, they were our neighbors."

"I remember that Tony had a crush on Joyce Wise all through high school," I said.

"You're an idiot, John. I only took her to the Junior and Senior Proms. That doesn't mean I had a crush on her or that we were even going steady. I was just being nice to the neighbor girl. You could call them mercy dates. Then, I found out she likes girls."

"Doesn't everybody?" I chided. "You were married to one … for a little while."

"Shut up, the both of you. What time is it anyway? Holy shit! It's two o'clock in the morning. I'm goin' to bed!" Dad bellowed.

Everything suddenly got quiet. I whispered to Tony that he could have my bed. I'd sleep on the couch. The next morning, the white hearse was waiting at the curb and the Wises' were walking to their cars.

"Geez," Dad complained, "can't they wait till we have our coffee?"

Both my dad and I were dressed in dark suits, white shirts and black neckties. In an act of helpfulness, Tony tied Dad's tie for him. "What the hell you doin,' Tony? Dad mumbled. "I thought I taught you how to tie a Winsor knot. Anybody can do a four-in-hand."

I opened the driver's side door of the Buick when my dad told me that Tony was driving. I slid into the backseat behind Dad. I looked at the backs of their heads and noted that they both were graying with matching bald spots.

My dad was giving Tony directions on how to get to Gem City when Tony interrupted. "I think I can just follow the hearse. He knows where to go."

I looked out the back window and the Wises' were right behind with their headlights on.

The Wise family had other reasons for going along, besides paying their respects. Ann's and Charlie's son, Tim was buried at Gethsemane Cemetery and they had also purchased plots for themselves. They were curious to see if their markers were in and what they looked like. Joyce and Cynthia still had to think about buying their own.

Moments after we headed out onto the highway, Dad's cigarette fell from his lips while he was talking to Tony. He panicked and yelled for Tony to pull over. Tony pulled to the shoulder, as did the rest of the convoy.

Tony scooped up the cigarette from Dad's lap. "It's not lit," Tony screamed. "Where's the cherry?"

"I think I found it," Dad wailed. "It's burning my nuts!" He slapped at his crotch with both hands.

Tony and I managed to get Dad out of the car and looked for a burn hole in his pants. There was only a small hole, and his suitcoat covered it. Tony seemed more concerned about the hole in the car seat. "Shit, Dad," Tony said, more than a little perturbed, "now, I'll have to get the thing re-covered."

Then, it dawned on me what the reason was for Tony's one-way ticket. He was getting the car and driving it back to Las Vegas. At that point, I truly didn't give a damn because I didn't want my dad to drive anymore. Besides, Tony's never moving back to Minnesota, and it wouldn't turn into a pile of rust in Nevada.

We all stopped for gas in a town preposterously named, Titan Town. It was only a fraction of the size of Gem City, but it had what we needed, gas, restrooms and a bar. The Wises' drove on ahead, but the three of us, plus the hearse driver, walked into the bar. It was called, the Nutty Squirrel.

We ordered dry martinis. I thought stopping for drinks, while Mom waited in the hearse, was highly inappropriate and voiced my concern. I was informed that we were only going to stay for one drink.

"Hey, you guys," I said. I motioned toward a sign on the wall, "this is a strip joint! Oh, never mind, the strippers don't come on till nine o'clock tonight."

We arrived at the cemetery fifteen minutes ahead of schedule. Reverend Erickson, six volunteer pallbearers, whom Erickson had recruited. The Wises' were sitting on metal folding chairs, alongside the casket.

With the casket in place, the service began. The Reverend, when he reached the part about, "ashes to ashes, dust to dust," took out a tiny glass vial of what looked like cigar ashes. The ashes didn't fall out as they were supposed to, so Erickson tapped the vial on the coffin lid. A little breeze came up and blew the ashes away. It may have been a metaphor for, "here today, gone tomorrow."

I choked back tears, remembering my mom was only fifty-four. She didn't have time to get any gray in her light blond hair.

Four cemetery workers waited patiently for us to leave the gravesite. They leaned against trees smoking cigarettes and glancing in our direction every few minutes. More obvious, was the orange crane, with the vault lid hoisted in the air, ready to move as soon as the last of the mourners left.

We didn't leave for quite a while.

38. No Rush Leaving a Cemetery

Following the graveside service, the Reverend and the pallbearers were the first to leave. The Wise family ambled toward their own gravesites to admire their new markers and to look at Tim Wise's grave.

My dad, Tony and I were still standing by Mom's casket, which rested above her yawning grave, when I overheard Dad whisper to Tony, "Would you look at that Charlie Wise? God, he must be proud of his walker."

"He can't help it," Tony whispered back, "he's got arthritis, you know."

"Yeah, I know," Dad said, louder than a whisper, "but still, he oughta get his hips and knees replaced, instead of using that stupid walker."

"How'd he get that way?" I asked Dad.

"From the ballpark, all that running, squatting and standing up fast."

"I didn't know he played baseball. "What position did he play? Catcher?"

"He didn't play baseball. He was a hotdog vendor."

I wanted to see if my dad's marker had been installed so I folded back part of the much-too-green outdoor carpet surrounding Mom's grave and found Dad's: FRANK J. ANDERSON WWII PVT. US ARMY. Dad came over, looked at it, snorted and walked away.

"The four of us," Dad muttered, "can't even be together in one place anymore."

"So, Tony, you don't want to be buried here? What are you gonna do?"

"If it's any of your business, John, I'm gonna be cremated and my ashes thrown from the top of Hoover Dam."

"Oh, good plan, Tony. That sounds like something you'd do."

"Hey, we gotta go," Dad yelled, as if Tony and I were hard of hearing. "Tony wants to go up to St. Stephen and transfer title on my car so he can head back to Nevada."

"Yeah, it's a long way and I have to go back to work."

"Why don't you guys go without me. I want to look around for a while. You can swing back and pick me up." Tony peered over his Ban-Rays and said that would be okay.

The hearse driver walked up and said, "I see that your buddies drove off without you. Tell you what, I'm going back to the Cities and I can give you a ride. You can ride in the back, now that it's empty."

I waved goodbye and said, "No thanks."

I noticed a young man leaning against the cemetery office building wearing jean cut-offs and a t-shirt, which I assumed used to be white. Where's Johnny Briggs? During a burial service, he usually stood, unobtrusively, nearby. He always wore a black suit that I found more appropriate than what this young man was wearing. Then it occurred to me, this kid was Briggs's assistant.

I approached him and asked where Mr. Briggs was. "He's dead," was his terse reply. "Died a couple months ago. Did you know that crazy old geek?"

"Crazy? What was crazy about him?" I started getting angry.

"Well, for one thing, the guy kept a .45 in the desk drawer. He thought gangsters were after him."

"Yeah," I responded defensively, "they were. Briggs once told me that, during prohibition, some of the big-time bootleggers thought he was encroaching on their territory and they came looking for him."

"And so," the punk added, sarcastically, "he decided to hide in Gem City. A black guy in Gem City would be sooo hard to find."

"Look, asshole," I explained, "first of all, they never saw him, didn't know what he looked like. Secondly, it's none of your business. Thirdly, what the hell are you doing here?"

"I'm the interim caretaker, until Fall semester begins at St. Cloud. You can have this job. I hate it. I'm never doing it again!"

"Doing what? You don't really do anything. Oh, yeah, you keep records. That's a real ball-buster. By the way, where's Mr. Briggs buried?"

"Next to the fence, in the corner. Briggs is over there."

I found Briggs's flat marble headstone and remembered him telling me that his age was a secret and I'd find out how old he was by looking at the dates chiseled into his tombstone. JOHN

HENRY BRIGGS. His middle name made perfect sense. Below his name: BORN: SEPT. 12, 1877; DIED: MARCH 1, 1975.

"Holy shit, man, ninety-eight!" I'd figured he was in his late seventies, or at least, in his early eighties.

I walked back to the office, so Dad and Tony could see me when they came back to pick me up. The mouthy kid had gone inside. I glanced over at my mom's casket once more. The workmen, thinking that I'd left began lowering her into the ground. I looked away.

We got home to Minneapolis in the early evening. Tony packed a few things and decided to leave that night instead of the next morning because he heard there would be rainstorms all day. I neglected to warn him that he'd be driving right into the storm system.

We said our goodbyes, gave him hugs and wished him a pleasant trip. "Tony, I hope things work out for your Hoover Dam plans."

My dad and I watched Tony drive away till the Buick's taillights faded into the darkness.

Dad seemed to have shrunk. His once broad shoulders looked thinner and closer together. I cooked for him and he only picked at his food, night after night. If he was depressed, I couldn't blame him. I was reminded of all the times my parents told me I had to clean my plate before leaving the table. It wouldn't be right to suggest it to him now.

39. Dad Checks Out

August after Mom died, I remember it was a Tuesday afternoon and so blistering hot at the foundry they let some of us go home early. Since starting to work there I'd lost twenty pounds. Every day I looked more bedraggled than the day before. I hurried home to have a drink with ice in it. I didn't care what it was. It could even be water.

I walked into the house, shouted to my dad, "I'm home."

He didn't hear because the damn TV was too loud, the *Love Boat* theme blasting. *How can he watch that crap, day after day?*

I found him sitting on the couch in the living room. At first, I thought he was taking a nap—alcohol induced probably—in front of the TV, which he usually did. But I could tell by his waxy pallor that he was gone. Dead. Horrifying.

I snapped off the TV and called the police to report a death in the home. Two beefy cops showed up and asked me if I wanted an autopsy performed. I said that I didn't, but I wanted my dad to have one. The cops looked at each other and frowned. One of them used our phone to call the coroner.

"Looks like he's been dead for a few hours," the other cop informed me. "Where were you when it happened?"

"I was at work." All of a sudden, guilt hit me like an eighteen-wheeler. *If I had only been home, this wouldn't have happened.* I was going crazy trying to reason with myself. *Why should I feel guilty? It's my job's fault.*

After the cops left and the coroner picked up my dad's body, I phoned the foreman at work and told him I wouldn't be back for at least two weeks. Then, I phoned Tony at the Golden Nugget and told him bluntly, "Dad died."

"What're you gonna do now, John? You've got to sell the house and send me half the money."

"There's no equity, Tony. It's mortgaged to the hilt. After the real estate agent's commission, I'll probably lose money. But if I decide to move on, I'll sell it.

"Are you coming back for Dad's funeral?"

"I'm a little strapped right now. Can you wire me the airfare?"

"Airfare? What about driving Dad's car up here?"

"I sold it."

"What? Then you must still have some money to pay for airfare. How much did you get for it? I think it was worth about nine-hundred, wasn't it?"

"The money's gone, John. The cost of living's a lot higher out here. I've got tons of expenses."

"I guess you won't be able to make it, then. Bye."

Satisfied with the brief conversation, I slammed down the receiver as hard as I could.

The next day, the coroner called and informed me of my dad's official cause of death. "Your father died of a hemorrhagic stroke."

40. Gethsemane Reprise

Black hearse. "Black is for boys," my Dad would have said. Me in front seat. No one else was going along to see that my old man received a proper burial. The day before burial, I viewed his body at the funeral home, dressed in the same suit, the one with the hole in the pants, that he wore the day my mother was buried.

The driver was a different guy, so I explained the family tradition of stopping in Titan Town at the Nutty Squirrel for refueling. Gas and liquor.

Reverend Erickson and the pallbearers met the hearse when we arrived at Gethsemane. The sun made a brief cameo appearance then quickly disappeared behind light drizzle. A canopy was setup at Dad's gravesite and the only person who spoke was the Reverend.

After the service, the pallbearers, followed by Reverend Erickson, walked away, leaving me standing there alone. Mom's prediction came eerily true. They had needed me to bury them. *Who's gonna bury me?* The hearse driver waited impatiently, revving the engine.

The driver told the same joke about offering me a ride in the back. Must be a mortuary thing. I just ignored him. "Go south on Main Street. There's something I wanna see."

I told him to slow down when St. Stephen Lutheran Church came into view. If we had stayed in Gem City, my parents would've had their funerals there, instead of burial services hardly anyone attended.

A large rectangular sign on the front lawn of the church announced Vacation Bible School would begin in two weeks. Vacation Bible School, three words that should never belong in the same sentence. To me, it seemed as if it was a device to squeeze the last breath out of what little remained of summer vacation's anarchy. My parents, mainly my mom, decided twelve years old would be the maximum age limit for Tony and me to attend Vacation Bible School.

But, for eight summers, before real school started, I glued rotini for beards on the faces of Abraham, Moses and a dozen more Old Testament look-alikes. One time, out of boredom, I glued some of the pasta on my own face. The Bible crafts teacher sent me home, where I incurred my mother's wrath.

I had the driver slow down when we came to Gene Dean's gas station. Gene had closed all his pumps. Outside the Qik Stop door, a sandwich sign which read, VISIT OUR NEW JAMES DEAN MUSEUM. ADMISSION: $8.50 PER PERSON. I guessed that it was part of the plan to rejuvenate Gem City.

We connected with the state highway and stopped again in Titan Town. When I finally got home to Minneapolis, I sat at the kitchen table with a tumbler full of ice cubes and Jack Daniel. It was quiet without the TV blaring.

A copy of the St. Stephen *Bulletin* lay on the table, opened to the page where I had left off. Under the headline, "Big Plans for Gem City!" the dutiful reporter regurgitated from a press release exactly the economic miracle that would occur in the very near future.

A thirty-mile gap of green space between St. Steven and Gem City would be filled with such things as a five-star luxury hotel, high-end condos, a multi-plex movie theater, a county museum, a city museum, a water park, a campground with all the amenities, a sports complex and an eighteen-foot, bronze statue of Father Louis Hennepin, the first white man to set foot on Gem City soil. Gem City's Gethsemane Cemetery would also be expanded to accommodate the growing needs of St. Stephen. The story also noted that Gem City Mayor Gene Dean would continue as a county employee, Mayor in name only, under the direction of County Commissioner Myron "Rocky" Sousé. I guess that made it official. Gem City was now a suburb of St. Stephen.

I turned to the help-wanted ads and found, not surprisingly, an opening for caretaker at Gethsemane Cemetery, a permanent county position salaried at $20,000 per year with free living quarters. Not bad. Everything like grass-cutting and grave-digging is contracted out. No wonder Johnny Briggs loved it. I really should check it out.

The phone rang. It was Tony. "How did Dad's burial go?"

"It went fine, Tony, but you still should've been there."

"Well, I couldn't be there." Tony took a deep breath. "What're your plans now, John?"

"I'm gonna sell the house and move back to Gem City where there might be an interesting job waiting for me."

"Interesting like what?"

"Cemetery caretaker."

"John, you don't wanna do that. That's a job for weirdos. Why don't you stay in the Cities, work and finish school?"

"No, my past and my future is in Gem City."

I held an estate sale while the house was being marketed. It only took three months to sell everything. I left for Gem City the day after closing. It didn't surprise me in the least that I had been hired for the job at Gethsemane. After all, I was almost a college graduate.

I found my new office and home a little too austere for my taste, but it was comfortably furnished in what looked like a depression-era motif. Satisfactory. I spent for first day on the job studying the signed contracts for new burial plots. Some would be fulfilled sooner than others.

I discovered it was true that Johnny Briggs kept a nickel-plated .45 semi-automatic with a walnut stock in his desk drawer. There were also two boxes of ammunition and an empty clip. I pushed seven stout bullets into the clip and slammed it into the gun with the palm of my hand. Two and a half pounds of lethal force in my fist, aptly nicknamed, "Man Stopper." That .45 would do more than just stop a man. I took off the safety and wondered if it was true that a person who was shot in the head wouldn't feel it, since the brain has no nerve endings. I carefully extracted the magazine and put the weapon back into the drawer.

After about a year on the job, I requisitioned the county for more grave diggers and a raise. They told me more workers would be available and even though I was doing a fine job, I couldn't have a raise yet.

One humid summer night, while watching TV, I heard some people talking and laughing outside. Knowing that it wasn't any of the cemetery tenants, I grabbed the .45, loaded the clip and stepped outside to find a group of six teenage boys. They'd tipped over two large tombstones and were starting on a third.

"Hold it right there!" I shouted, holding the gun behind my back, "What in the hell do you piss ants think you're doing?"

"Well, who the fuck are you?" One of them yelled back.

"I am," I stated calmly, "the guardian of the Pantheon this side of the River Styx."

They laughed and yelled, "What'd you say, you crazy bastard?"

I ignored their taunts and told them to put the tombstones back into place. "Then you can go home." They refused and stood their ground. "Look," I said, "I'm not offended by your sociopathic behavior, but my associate, Colonel Colt, is truly upset."

Holding the gun with two hands, I fired off a round in the air. The noise was deafening. I could hardly hear their fearful screams. "Pick those goddam tombstones up, right now!" I ordered, as I leveled the gun on them. They were crying and probably, involuntarily losing control of their bladders and bowels. After they straightened up the headstones, they ran off into the night, still screaming and crying.

In the years that followed, I was content with my job and my life. Occasionally, vandals would come into the cemetery bent on unholy desecration. Whenever they did, however, they were promptly introduced to my friend, the Colonel, who would, in his own inimitable way, tell them what they were doing was wrong.

When the new century dawned, I looked at the calendar, then looked in the mirror. *My god. I'm not as old as Johnny Briggs, but I sure look like I am.*

A true jazz connoisseur, Briggs had a stack of well-worn 78 rpm records, mostly those of Art Tatum. Like Briggs, I whiled away lonely evenings listening to those jazz, especially in the winter. In the winter, the sun makes a lazy arc across the south, goes to bed early, sleeps late and its heat is hardly enough to melt away the wispiest of clouds.

41. Tony Cashes in His Chips

Being a cemetery caretaker wasn't such a bad job. People often told me that, even though they said they'd never do it themselves, "Yes, it's a good job, easy enough." I was in it for life, just like Johnny Briggs, the Pope and William O. Douglas.

In the summertime, on a still night, I'd look out on the cemetery grounds and could see yellow-greenish clouds rising from the graves of the recently interred. When I first saw this specter, I foolishly thought it was the spirits of the deceased, but when a chemist explained that it was only gas from the natural chemicals in a person's body that caused the phenomenon, I feigned nonchalance. I was quite happy whenever this occurred because it always scared would-be vandals away.

I'd sometimes have trouble with these teenage vandals, even after I had motion triggered security lighting installed, which illuminated almost the entire cemetery. The little shits still try to sneak in. I actually came to enjoy running outside and shouting with my trusty .45 raised above my head.

Winter, however, was a different story. The "fair-weather freaks," as I called them, usually stayed away. When winter came, I usually got lonely with little else to do except for the occasional county worker to supervise, who, when it was below-zero, thawed the ground with a cylindrical, grave-sized, steel propane tank. The county had two ground thawers. Around Christmastime one winter, I learned I was to be the last surviving member of my family. Midge, my brother's girlfriend when he died of congestive heart failure, called me collect with news.

"Your brother is dead, John."

Tony and I, in later years, weren't the best of friends, not even the best of brothers, but hearing the crushing news was like driving a Ford Pinto, being rear-ended by a Lincoln Towncar and getting incinerated when the gas tank blows up.

I asked Midge if there was going to be a probate hearing. She said there wouldn't be because after Tony retired, he gambled and drank away what little money remained.

"Wait a minute, Midge. I thought showgirls made a lot of money."

"Who told you I was a showgirl?"

"Tony."

"I wasn't. I'm a cashier at the Golden Nugget."

She explained that according to his wishes, he was cremated, and she poured his ashes from the observation deck at Hoover Dam.

A person's life and history reduced to a pile of ashes and poured from a one-pound coffee can.

I recalled Christmases past, when Tony and I would laugh and talk about the Christmas cards our parents sent out to their friends and relatives, most of whom we'd never met. They had kept the tradition going until people died and were scratched off the list. The list eventually dwindled down, after forty or so years, to only a few names.

After my parents and Tony died, I thought about continuing the tradition, but hell, I didn't know these people, so it stopped. It had also occurred to me that if I didn't send any cards, I wouldn't get any either. Tony and I never sent Christmas cards to anyone, not even each other.

It was plain to see that the coming Christmas would be no different unless I did something about it. So I did. I had no relatives, no wife, girlfriend, not even any live friends. I began looking through the Minneapolis phonebook and picked out the first thirty people named Anderson. They would get Christmas cards from me. I also thought it would be fun to include a newsletter about my family, which would, of course, be entirely fictionalized.

"Dear friends and relatives," it began, "We hope you're doing well at this most blessed time of the year. Just to keep you up to date on what our family's been doing, I'll offer this brief synopsis: My lovely wife, Heather, has recently completed her third novel, "The Christmas Camel," a children's story about a camel who was present at the birth of Christ. While working on her writing projects, she also received her Ph.D. in child psychology. What a gal! We're also proud of our daughter, Tiffany, who graduated last year, Magna Cum Laude from Harvard Law School. After she marries her law professor, she plans to specialize in trial law, just like her daddy. What are you folks up to, these days? Be sure to drop us a line. It'll be wonderful hearing from you. All our best, John J. Anderson."

A few days, perhaps a week after I mailed the cards to the

Anderson families, three people replied, saying they never heard of me and asked that their names be removed from my Christmas card list. Next year, I'll mail out twenty-seven.

42. Public Enemy Number One

One evening, listening to a Coleman Hawkins L.P., I started reminiscing about a story my dad had told me when I was sixteen.

"When I was your age," he began, "there was a rumor that John Dillinger himself, was planning to drive through Gem City on Main Street. There were questions whether or not Police Chief Roy Troutfedder was up to the task. Roy had a bum leg. Picked up some shrapnel during World War One. I remember Mayor Joe Beemish was against Troutfedder becoming Police Chief in the first place. He complained that Roy was a German. Ada Nesterud lit into the Mayor saying that Roy had fought on our side in the Great War, as they called it back then. And there was German shrapnel in his leg. Got a purple heart for it, too."

Thanks to Dad's story, I picked up little bits about Dillinger over the years. The entire country was glued to their radios to hear about the escapades and escapes of Public Enemy Number One, John Herbert Dillinger. It started in March of 1934 when he escaped from the escape proof Crown Point Jail in Indiana. He then escaped from the clutches of the FBI at a lodge in Northern Wisconsin called, Little Bohemia, and from a hotel in St. Paul after a lengthy gun battle with police.

In the middle of June of that year, Chief Troutfedder received a phone call from FBI Special Agent in charge, Melvin Purvis. Purvis explained that Dillinger was rumored to be headed North from the Twin Cities, and that he might try to pass through Gem City, in which case, Troutfedder was ordered to take him, "dead or alive." Better dead than alive. This would be Roy's baptism by fire. He hung up the phone, mustered his police force, and deputized a few more men.

Just so happened that same morning the FBI called Roy, Mayor Beemish happened to look out his second-story office window in City Hall and noticed several police officers dragging sawhorses across Main Street. He ran down the steps and out into the street. His wife, Eunice, also the council secretary, ran behind with a pencil and steno pad.

Troutfedder was talking to one of the officers when he heard the footfalls of the Mayor. He turned to see Beemish, red-faced, arms waving. "Aw geez," the Chief groaned, turning back to his conversation with his officer.

"Chief, Chief Troutfedder!" the Mayor shouted. Troutfedder turned slowly to face him. "What the hell's the meaning of this? What's going on here?" Eunice was taking notes furiously as the Chief explained the call from Purvis.

"Well," demanded Beemish, "why wasn't I informed?"

"It just slipped my mind, sir. Now for your own and Mrs. Beemish's safety, would you please go back inside?" Troutfedder motioned toward City Hall.

Citizens began to gather on the sidewalks when they had heard the rumors that Johnny Dillinger was coming to Gem City. High School kids carried signs which proclaimed, "Gem City Welcomes John Dillinger!"

"Take those signs away," Mayor Beemish ordered, "and get those kids back in school. Who do they think he is, Charles Lindbergh? The man's a criminal, a killer!" Troutfedder told his men to clear the area and to keep crowds from forming.

Both ends of Main Street were blocked with heavily armed men at both positions. The police hoped that Dillinger would turn down one of the side streets into a dead end. There was a mood of excitement for this was the biggest event ever to hit Gem City.

"Troutfedder, how the hell do you think you few men are gonna stop Dillinger, when the FBI and everybody else couldn't do it? What's your plan? Are your men experienced enough? Are they brave enough to take on John Dillinger?"

"Look Mr. Mayor, these men, most of 'em, including myself, fought the Hun in France during the Great War. If they could save the world for Democracy, they can save Gem City from the likes of John Dillinger. He'll be sorry he even thought of driving through here. Do you understand? Now, go back to your office and stay there. We've got a job to do and you're in the way."

"You can't talk to me that way! I'll have your badge!"

"I'd suggest, sir, that you talk to Mrs. Nesterud about that."

The police stayed at their posts in around-the-clock shifts for about a week. No John Dillinger. The men killed time by cleaning their pistols and shotguns. Occasionally, a couple of them- drove a few miles out of town for target practice.

On the morning of June 23, 1934, Gem City and the rest of the country heard the radio news; the night before, John Dillinger had been surrounded by Purvis' FBI agents and gunned down in front of the Biograph Theater in Chicago.

Chief Troutfedder was furious. He dismissed his detail and had the roadblocks taken down. His hands were shaking when he phoned Melvin Purvis. "You assholes," yelled the Chief, "couldn't you have the professional courtesy to call and tell us you got him in Chicago?"

Word spread around Gem City that their police chief had stood up to Purvis as well as FBI Director John Edgar Hoover.

The citizens of Gem City rewarded Roy Troutfedder by electing him Mayor the following November.

My dad's version of the story even topped the one where he won World War Two singlehandedly. I believed that Dillinger was thinking about cruising through Gem City. A few locals who were around at the time, corroborated it.

43. The Ballad of Lorton & Floyd

My great-uncles, Lorton and Floyd, made a rare visit to Gem City when I was nine, so that would make it, 1956. They were my dad's uncles, and lived together in Sioux Rapids, Iowa. That's where my dad was born. They explained that they were on vacation and thought they'd stop in and say, "Hi." When I was nine, I couldn't imagine anyone from anywhere wanting to spend part of their vacation in Gem City.

"We'll be spending at least two days with you," announced Floyd.

"If that's all right with you?" said Lorton.

There was something I couldn't quite figure out about them, besides why they stopped in Gem City. They were both only about ten years older than my dad. My other great-aunts and uncles were my grandparents' age. Lorton and Floyd, after two divorces each and true to their eccentricities, took a vow of bachelorhood and remained single for the rest of their lives. Struck me as wacko.

An oft repeated story about them, which my dad told with added pejoration, concerned the time these lunatic uncles robbed a gas station. Now, they were in our living room and I wanted to hear that story again, the true story, this time, from their own lips.

"Johnny," Lorton said, "you don't want to hear that old story again, do you?"

"Yeah, of course I do." I answered.

Lorton looked at Floyd and said, "Can you believe that Floyd here, wanted to be called, Pretty Boy Floyd? Just look at 'im. He ain't pretty at all. Never was."

"You gonna tell the story, or should I?" grumbled Floyd.

"Okay, okay. I was nineteen and Floyd was twenty-one," Lorton began. "It was 1932, during the Great Depression. We both lost our jobs at the feed mill and thank god, we were still living at home with our mother, otherwise we wouldn't have had a place to live. Anyway, we got drunk one night. ..."

"... On some cheap shine," Floyd added, "'cause it was Prohibition, you know."

"Yeah," Lorton said, "and it was the last dollar we had between us. So, on a hot, stinkin' August night ... geez, there wasn't no breeze. And humid? Kee-rist! We were gonna get up real early and rob the gas station, but as it turned out, we didn't get up till noon and we were so hungover we couldn't hardly navigate."

My brother Tony, who was listening in the other room, snapped off the TV and he and my dad joined in to listen. My mom, who'd heard the story countless times, was busy making up the hide-a-bed.

"Since it was my plan and I'm the oldest, I'll start the story," Floyd said.

My dad was already rolling his eyes, while Tony and I sat attentively.

"'Well, Lort, this is it,' I says. 'Get dressed. We're gonna go rob the gas station.'"

"'Floyd,' Lort says to me, 'I just don't know about this. Do ya know who's gonna be workin' there?'"

"'Yeah, some dumb kid, that's all.'"

"'What if there's no money in the till? I mean, ya know, times bein' the way they are.'"

"'C'mon, it's the only gas station in town. There's bound to be some money. Think of it this way, prosperity's just around the corner for us.'"

"'Yeah, that's what President Hoover says, and he's the one who got us into this mess to begin with.'"

"'I think that we'll bring Dad's gun, the one from the War.'"

"'Dad wasn't in the War.'"

"'I know, stupid,' I says, a little perturbed by my brother's constantly questioning me. "The gun was in the war.'"

"'What if that kid's got a gun under the counter?'"

"'We'll come in with our gun out right away and make 'im put his hands up.'"

"'We don't even know if that old gun works and besides, we don't have any bullets.'"

"'The kid won't know that. It don't matter anyway, because we're not actually gonna shoot 'im, ya know.'"

"'And then what, Floyd? Okay, say we get the money, we start to make our getaway and the kid calls the cops?'"

"'Before we go in, we can cut the telephone line. Use the jackknife I gave ya for yer birthday.'"

"'I sold it.'"

"'Then use mine, for god sakes.'"

"'That's all fine and good, but how do we make our getaway without a car? Do we just start runnin'?'"

"'Lort, if we start runnin', we'll draw suspicion. There's a cornfield nearby, so we can slowly walk into it.'"

"'Floyd, I really don't think we need the money that bad. I mean, we could get caught. I seen the police chief's car there, lottsa times. He always stops there for gas.'"

"'Aw, ya chickenshit! Some partner you are. I guess I hafta do this myself.'"

"'No, no. I'll go along, but only to be the lookout. You go in with the gun and I'll cut the phone wire, okay?'"

"Well," said Floyd looking around to make sure everybody was listening. "we pulled that heist. Our first and only crime, and we got eight dollars and thirty-five cents. You can't divide that, but since I did most of the work, I got the extra penny. As we were walkin' to the cornfield, nonchalant as possible, wouldn't you know it but the police chief pulls alongside and says, 'Well, if it ain't Lorton and Floyd. Gimme the gun and get in the backseat.' I tried to shuffle the gun to Lorton, but he refused to take it, so I had to take most of the blame."

Lorton nodded and said, "Yeah, the judge gave Floyd ninety days in the workhouse and gave me sixty days. I told the judge that it was just as much my fault and that I should get ninety days, too. You know, that little judge just smiled and agreed with me. So, it was ninety days for the both of us. I guess we should've headed to Linn Grove where there's more places to hide."

"Did you ever find out who called the police?"

"Yeah," Floyd answered, "it was our grandmother. She overheard us planning the robbery."

"Hey, Lorton," my dad asked, "soon after that, didn't you become a cop in Storm Lake?"

"Yeah," Lorton replied. "I felt so bad about what happened, and I wanted to prove that I wasn't no Bonnie and Clyde, so I became a cop. Made it to Lieutenant before I retired."

Dad, Tony and I looked at each other, and I said, "Boy, that's sure a different story than how Dad tells it."

Tony jabbed me in the ribs with his elbow.

44. Meeting Ms. Clarke

When I awoke one Saturday, there was nothing for me to do but wait for Mayor Dean's liquor store to open. His wife would serve out her two-year term as the current mayor, then Gene could run unopposed and resume his lofty position.

Gene's store slogan read, "Proudly serving the people of Gem City for One-eighth of a Century!"

At first, some folks were skeptical of sharing information with Gene, the town gossip who they talked to nearly every day.

Gene would ask, "How's it goin'?"

People would say, "Fine," or "Horseshit." In either case, he would probe till he found the reason why they felt that way.

I had planned to go to the liquor store and get a quart of forgetfulness when the phone rang. I should've unplugged the phone the night before. It was Gene's wife, Mayor Natalie Dean.

"Listen, John, there'll be a young lady named Kim Clarke who'll be coming to see you in a few minutes."

"What the hell for?"

"We've got plans to turn the cemetery building into a funeral chapel and she can help us facilitate that. She has a degree from the community college in Mortuary Science, then she'll be going to Saint Cloud for her Bachelor's. And after that, she'll be the new funeral director."

"What happened to the old funeral directors?"

"One died. The other one is close to retirement and when he retires, Ms. Clarke will move in."

"You mean literally?"

"Yes, of course."

"But, I'm the caretaker. Where'll I go?"

"You're gonna find someplace else to live, I guess. Besides, you don't actually do anything. Your job title should be Night Watchman. Anyway, get ready to meet Ms. Clarke. She should be there in about ten minutes. I hope you haven't been drinking, have you? You sound slurry."

"No, I just got up. What does this Ms. Clarke look like?"

"It doesn't matter. You're not her type, anyway."

"How do you know? Doesn't she like men who're alive and standing up?"

"She doesn't like men, period."

At that very moment, Gene would be unlocking the doors of his liquor store to a half-dozen customers who were patiently waiting in the parking lot.

I gazed in the bathroom mirror and didn't like the face staring back at me. I looked ten years older than I actually was. Thought about shaving and sprucing up a bit but decided not to. So, I ran a comb through thinning hair and splashed some cold water in my face. It didn't, however, fix my watery, bloodshot eyes. Besides, I wasn't her type.

I'd only finished getting dressed when Ms. Clark knocked on my door.

"Hi, I'm Kim Clarke, nice to meet you."

"John Anderson. Is Kim short for Kimberly?"

"Yes, but call me Kim."

"Okay, because when I say, Kimberly Clarke, it reminds me of toilet paper."

"I said, call me Kim and I mean it."

"Oh, yes Ma'am."

Right away, we were off to a bad start.

"So, I guess you'll be kicking me out of my home. I'll have to look for an apartment somewhere. I wonder if I'll have to find another job, too."

"But you don't really do anything. The county sends people to cut the grass and dig graves."

"I use the weed-whacker around the standing monuments."

"Big deal."

"The phone's ringing. I'd better answer it. Probably the Mayor wanting to hear how we're getting along. Ha, ha!" I picked up the receiver.

"Hello, John? It's Gene. Natalie probably didn't tell you, but we've decided to downsize a bit."

"What do ya mean by that?"

"First of all, Ms. Clark'll be taking over your job as caretaker. It's a money thing. So, we're going to retire you. The good news is you'll be able to collect a pension, a good-sized one, as a county employee. And that should last you for the rest of your life. Just don't leave Gem City. I appreciate your loyal patronage at my store and, of course, your vote at election time."

I thanked him and told Ms. Clarke that I had a very important appointment, and it would take several hours.

"Let's do this some other time, okay?" I lied. I never wanted to see her unwrinkled face, again.

What did Kimberly Clarke know about Gem City or Gethsemane? Absolutely nothing and it wouldn't even occur to her to ask me.

If I moved back to Minneapolis, Gem City would eventually draw me back like a magnet. I don't exactly know why. It also crossed my mind to move to St. Stephen, but I decided that Gem City, no matter what, would call me back, because years ago I purchased a burial plot sandwiched between my dad and my mother.

Acknowledgements

Thank you, Tom Driscoll for your patience, belief in me and for giving me a chance from the very beginning.

About the Author

J.P. Johnson continues to be a retired real estate agent from Northeast Minneapolis and is still writing. He has previously published two short story collections: *Convoluted Tales* and *Convoluted Tales 2.0*.

www.ingramcontent.com/pod-product-compliance
Lightning Source LLC
Chambersburg PA
CBHW051124260626
47170CB00005B/1652